The Making of a Man

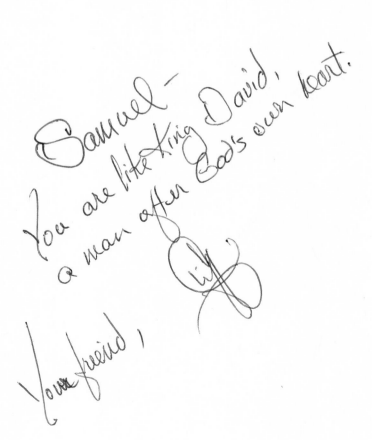

Samuel –

You are like King David,

a man after God's own heart.

Your friend,

The Making of a Man

What Are Little Boys Made Of?

Cliff LeCleir

Library of Congress Control Number: 2013913437
ISBN: Hardcover   978-1-4836-7394-3
                 Softcover   978-1-4836-7393-6
                 Ebook   978-1-4836-7395-0

This book was printed in the United States of America.

Rev. date: 08/07/2013

To order additional copies of this book, contact:
email: clifflecleir@gmail.com
or
Xlibris LLC
1-888-795-4274
www.Xlibris.com
Orders@Xlibris.com
135108

Contents

Names of Characters

Bertram, Lowell	Lead designer hired away from the Brown Shoe Co.
Buchanan, Dinah	Rob & Henrika's daughter
Buchanan, Henrika	Robs wife, Gustave's daughter, Elsa's sister
Buchanan, Robert (Rob)	Sales & Marketing Mgr. for the Walk-On Shoe Co., friend & brother-in-law to Tomas
Buchanan, Rueben	Rob & Henrika's oldest son
Buchanan, Simon	Rob & Henrika's 2nd son
Camacho, Carlos	Presidente Turbay's minister of security, purchaser of Joseph, friend of Escobar
Carl	Kelley's brother
Escobar, Pablo	Pablo Emilio Escobar Gaviria, a famous, weathy drug lord
Felipe	The president's Usher who was in prison with Joseph
Gus	Nightwatchman at The Leather Werks
Julio Cesar Turbay Ayala	President of Columbia
Kelley	Neighbor girl across the street from the Buchanan's
Liddell, Harvey	Driver of the Co-op gas truck
McConnell, Ace	Head Foreman at Walk-On Shoe Co.
Moravec, Joe	Promoted to Sales Manager at The Leather Werks
Ostergren, Orley	Gustave's lead designer
Pederson, Pastor Bill & wife Ruby	Pastor of the Chapel, a community Bible church

Pritchard, Conrad & Evelyn	M&I Banker and his wife
Radar	The Leather Werks watchdog
Renner, Geroge-wife Rosemary	A VP & long-time valued employee of The Leather Werks
Soderstrom, Elsa	Gustave's youngest daughter, married Tomas
Soderstrom, Gustave	Becca's brother
Soderstrom, Henrika	Gustave's oldest daughter, married Rob
Soderstrom, Mikkel	Gustave's oldest son
Soderstrom, Nicolai	Gustave's younest son
Tryggestad, Howard-wife Myrna	A VP & long-time valued employee of The Leather Werks
Zurbriggen, Becca	Zachary's wife
Zurbriggen, Benjamin	Tomas' youngest son
Zurbriggen, Joseph	Tomas' 2nd youngest son
Zurbriggen, Marcus	Zachary eldest twin son
Zurbriggen, Massses	The family patriarch & founder of The Leather Werks
Zurbriggen, Sarah	Masses wife
Zurbriggen, Tomas	Zachary youngest twin son
Zurbriggen, Zachary	Masses & Sarah's son

INTRODUCTION

I N THE NINETEENTH century, a series of children's rhymes were circulating entitled *Mother Goose Nursery Rhymes*. One such rhyme was called "What Are Little Boys Made Of?" It went like this:

> **"What are little boys made of?**
> **Snips and snails, and puppy dogs tails**
> **That's what little boys are made of!**
> **What are little girls made of?**
> **Sugar and spice and all things nice**
> **That's what little girls are made of!"**

You, my dear reader, are going on a journey that will provide a privileged view into the life of Tomas Zurbriggen, the central character in this story. You will observe the process of Tomas growing from a boy into a man. It is during this process that you will not only learn what this boy was made of but also what it took to make him into a man.

Tomas became a striking figure as he matured. He was tall and handsome, had dark chiseled features, black hair, and snapping black eyes. His temperament displayed a mixture of characteristics: charming yet deceitful, contemplative while manipulative. Tomas did everything, both right and wrong, with great zeal – a trait that if not harnessed would become his downfall.

His grandfather Masses Zurbriggen, a good, morally solid Swiss gentleman and a tanner by trade, had migrated to America from Switzerland in 1907. He made his living processing animal hides into leather and crafting the leather into articles in demand: belts, harnesses, straps, aprons, holsters, and other materials of necessity. His marriage to Sarah, whom he called Princess, produced one son, Zachary, who joined his father in the business and expanded their line of products into fine leather coats.

Zachary was a carbon copy of his father. They looked alike, thought alike, and had the same moral foundation. Zachary found himself captivated by Becca, a young American girl who became his loving and loyal wife, if one would overlook her tendency to be a bit manipulative.

Zachary and Becca's union produced twin boys who were polar opposite of each other. Tomas, whose name means "twin," was the second to be born. His brother, Marcus, grew up to be big boned, ruddy complexioned, and a lover of the outdoors.

It is with this heritage that we begin to observe . . .

the making of a man.

CHAPTER 1

The Signing

IN 1960, THE dad-son team of Masses and Zachary Zurbriggen had expanded their business and their distribution sufficiently to warrant a move from the converted cow barn on Masses homestead in rural Cadott, Wisconsin, to a larger facility. They decided on a property in Chippewa Falls, a larger town fifteen miles east of where Masses had begun nearly fifty years before.

It was now 1966, and the move had proved to be very successful. Zachary had implemented a new product line of fine leather coats, and his promotion of that product, along with a superb reputation for quality, saw their sales increase exponentially. His innovation was timely, for the company's original products had exhausted their use and had literally gone the way of the *"buggy whip."* Masses was now retired, and Zachary assumed the role of company president, after they incorporated under the name of Zurbriggen Leather Werks.

Zachary's twin boys, Marcus and Tomas, were sophomores in college now, but during summers and holidays, they worked in the family business. Zachary felt everyone should contribute to their livelihood and not have a sense of entitlement, especially his boys. Besides, as he often affirmed, he was grooming them to assume leadership in the company someday. Once they entered college, he put them under the tutelage of two of the company's vice presidents, Marcus under George Renner in production control, and Tomas under Howard Tryggestad in sales.

* * *

It was late Friday afternoon, and everyone had left for the weekend. Everyone, except Tomas, who was just finishing his weekly sales report when the phone rang. Concentrating on completing the number he was writing, his hand fumbled for the receiver.

"Zurbriggen Leather Werks sales office, Tomas speaking."

"Tom, this is Marc."

"Hey, bro, how did the fishing trip go?"

"Tom, I need your help. I'm in jail."

"What? Where? Marc, what's going on?"

"I'm in the Barron County Jail. Tom, it's going to take $240 to get me out of here. Can you dig up that much?"

"Don't you have the money, Marc?"

"No. Can you loan me the cash? I'll pay you back."

"Well, uh, sure, but what in the dickens is going on?"

"Listen, I have only one phone call, and I have to go. This jailer is signaling for me to get off the line. Can you come right away? And, Tom, keep this between you and me, okay? Please, don't tell Dad!"

"How am I going to keep this from him? He finds out everything."

"Promise me you'll get up here now. Make up some excuse for going out of town, promise me!"

"All right, all right, I promise."

"I have to go. Uh, Tommy, thanks!"

Tomas hung up the phone and sat back in his chair. For several moments, he pondered the situation, wondering what his brother had got himself into; then an idea popped into his head.

This may turn into an opportunity, he thought as he pulled out a piece of company letterhead and began to write. When he finished, he picked up the phone and called home.

"Hello," answered the voice on the other end.

"Hi, Mom, this is Tom. Say, would it be okay if I stayed over at a friend's house tonight? You didn't have anything special planned, did you?"

"No, we have nothing planned. I guess it would fine. In fact, maybe I'll use the excuse of having both of you boys away to get your father to take me out to dinner."

"Oh, that sounds like a winner. I'll see you tomorrow then. Good night."

Tomas gathered his things, locked the office, and walked out across to the parking lot to his '41 Ford coupe. "Well, ole girl," he said affectionately as he ran his hand across the front fender, "you're going to have to get me up to Barron and back. I hope you're up for it."

As he headed for the gas station to fill the tank, he thought, *"I better stop by the Northwestern Bank and get some cash. The jail may not accept checks."*

Gassed up and with money in his pocket, Tomas headed north out of town, still wondering what harebrained stunt his brother could have pulled to get him thrown behind bars.

*   *   *

Barron was about forty miles from Chippewa Falls, and at eight o'clock, Tomas pulled in front of the Barron County Jail. He got out of the car and stood, looking at the brick structure before him, feeling a twinge of embarrassment that his brother was arrested and put in jail. Walking up to a massive oak door, he pulled it open, revealing a shoulder-high desk with a police officer sitting behind it. The room had an old, stuffy smell. From eye height to the ceiling, the walls were covered with dark oak panels. Where the oak left off, marble continued down the walls and continued across the floor.

"What can I do for you, young fella?" the policeman behind the desk asked.

"I've come to see my brother."

"Visiting hours was over an hour ago. You can come back tomorrow."

"Yes, sir, but I drove up from Chippewa to get him out."

The policeman stroked his chin as he sized up the young man in front of him. "What's his name?" he asked.

"Marcus. Marcus Zurbriggen."

A few moments passed as the policeman thumbed through pages in a book.

"Oh, here he is, yes, Zurbriggen. You aren't going to get him out tonight though. Bail and fines can only be collected when the office staff is here during business hours. That would be from eight to five. Oh, wait a minute, that's during the week. Let me check and see what we do on weekends."

The officer returned shortly with another officer and said, "You're in luck, Officer Bentworth here is certified to accept payment of fines, but not bail. I see here your brother can be released if his fine is paid."

Officer Bentworth interjected, "Payment has to be made by cash or a certified bank draft, though."

"I have the cash, but can I see my brother first?"

"No. If you're paying the fine, it must be paid before contact."

"If I pay the fine, can I talk with him before he is processed out?"

The police officers looked at one another as if that was the first time they had ever heard such a request and then said, "I guess so."

Tomas counted out two hundred and forty dollars, received his receipt, and was led down a series of hallways through a door of sliding bars to the visitors' area.

Marcus was led into the room and seated at a table with Tomas.

"Tom," Marcus blurted out. "Thanks for coming, man."

Tomas threw his leg over the seat of a picnic-bench-style visitor's table and said, "How about a little explanation? What did you do?"

Marcus lowered his eyes in embarrassment and began to explain, "We were fishing on a lake north of here. About two hours after dark, we decided to go into town and grab something to eat. Some of the guys wanted to have a drink first, so we stopped at this bar."

"I suppose you were the only one trying to influence your buddies against that," Tomas said sarcastically.

Marcus just shrugged his shoulders and continued, "There were some locals in the bar bragging about their catch, and one of my buddies asked them where they were fishing. They said they were over at Breezy Point. My buddy said, 'That's funny. We were fishing at Breezy Point all day till after dark, and there was no one else in the area.' This guy gets all bent and stands up with his chest puffed out and said, 'Ya callin' me a liar?' My buddy said, 'No, I just think you're a geographic idiot!' Some pushing and shoving began, and when the local started getting the bad end of the deal, his buddies jumped on my friend. I wasn't about to let three guys pile on one, so I stepped up and with a couple of quick rights and lefts, sent the two of them flying."

"So the rest of them are in jail as well?" Tomas asked.

"Well, ah . . . no."

"Then explain something to me, Marc. You didn't start the fight. You just stopped the other two from entering the fight, but you're the only one in jail. Something isn't adding up."

"I guess it's because the two I sent flying crashed through a couple of windows. The bar owner swore out an arrest warrant, and until the damage is covered, and since I was the one sending them through the window . . ."

"Marcus, I don't know what to say. This is just plain dumb! You know Dad doesn't approve of these places." He got up as if to leave and said, "Oh, forget it. It's useless trying to talk to a bonehead like you."

"Wait a minute, bro. Aren't you going to get me out of here?"

"I don't know, Marc. Maybe it would do you some good to sit awhile and think about the consequences."

"Hey, I don't need a lecture."

"What do you need, Marc? What will pound sense into that thick skull of yours?"

"Anything, Tom, please. I'll pay you back. I'll double it. Just get me out of here. I'll do anything."

"You'll do anything, huh?" Tomas hesitated for a moment before saying, "Well, how about this. You know Dad favors you to take over the company someday."

"Ya, it seems that's his plan," Marcus admitted.

"How about this as payment to bail your butt outa here? If and when the head job is ever offered, you formally refuse to take it."

Marcus puckered his lips and, with an incredulous sneer, said, "What are you getting at? My refusal won't mean anything if Dad has his mind made up?"

"Here's the deal, Marc. If you sign away that right, I'll pay the fine, and you won't owe me a cent."

"You want me to sign something?"

"It's the only way I can tell if you're serious."

Without hesitation, Marcus replied, "Okay, sure, if it will get me out of this rattrap."

Tomas pulled a piece of paper from his pocket and said, "Here, read this and we'll see. If you agree to these terms, I'll bail you out."

Marcus took the paper and began to read.

Zurbriggen Leather Werks
        101 Bridge St., Chippewa Falls, Wisconsin

I, Marcus Zurbriggen, being of sound mind and body, on this 18th day of June, 1966, after receiving the sum of two hundred and forty dollars ($240), do hereby unequivocally revoke and refuse any right and/or claim to the title of president, chief executive officer, or other title signifying final authority in the company of the Zurbriggen Leather Werks, if such a position is offered at any time in the future, whether said business may be operating under the foregoing name or a name invoked due to legal or personal preferences of the principles.

_____   _____
    Name of signor   Date

Marcus finished reading the paper and threw it on the table. "Well," Tomas asked.

Marcus gave Tomas a disgusted look and said, "Sure. Who cares? Dad's going to put whomever he wants in charge. This won't make a difference one way or another. Give me a pen. I'll sign your blasted paper."

CHAPTER 2

A Week Earlier

THE FAMILY HAD just returned from Sunday services. Zachary collected the paper and retired to the living room. Becca busied herself by putting the finishing touches on their dinner. As she pulled the beef roast from the oven, she called upstairs to her sons.

"Boys, get your clothes changed and come and set the table for me."

A loud scuffling was going on in the boys' bedrooms, typical of the way brothers work off excess energy after sitting through an hour of Sunday school and another hour of church.

"Zachary!" Becca called to receive reinforcement from her husband.

Without looking up from his paper, Zachary called out, "Boys!"

"Yes, Pa, we're coming," they answered as the two slid down the banister, landing one on top of the other at the bottom of the stairs.

Becca, with her typical short, quick steps, walked through to the dining room laden with dishes of food and said, "You rascals will be the death of me yet. Now get washed and help set the table."

The family sat down for dinner, and Zachary offered a prayer to God, thanking him for His goodness to them and for blessing them with such a splendid meal.

He turned and addressed Marcus, "Tell me, son, after you pass over those mashed potatoes, what did you think was the most meaningful point in Pastor Peterson's sermon today?"

Marcus looked at his dad with a blank expression and said, "Uh?"

Tomas, obviously enjoying his brother's dilemma, said with mocking tones, "Marc, could you be a little more specific?"

Zachary, not seeing the humor in his son's lack of attention to the pastor's sermon, directed the question to his other son. "Since you are apparently so interested, Tomas, perhaps you could provide the answer."

Becca intervened and said, "Zachary, let's just have a quiet dinner without an interrogation for a change."

Tomas put on a serious expression, cleared his throat, and responded, "That's all right, Mom. From what I gathered, Pastor Peterson was explaining that there are two conflicting theological schools of thought in Christendom. He called them Arminianism and Calvinism. The former having to do with free will. Calvinism, on the other hand, states man's condition is in total depravity, and only the elect or the chosen will be preserved for eternity."

Zachary raised his eyebrows in surprise at the answer and asked, "How in tarnation did you remember all that, son?"

With a flippant air in his voice, Tomas answered, "I take notes."

Shaking his head in disbelief, Zachary said, "Very good, Tomas, but do you understand what you just said?"

Without hesitation, Tomas responded, "Not a word of it, but neither did Pastor Peterson."

"Oh! What makes you say that?"

"'Cause at the end he was struggling to complete the explanation and finally threw up his hands and said, 'I guess that makes me a Calminian.'"

That brought a chuckle from Zachary as he pondered the difficulty man has in grasping God's principles. He replied, "Boys, church fathers have been debating those views for centuries. I don't imagine that we are going to gain complete understanding here at our dinner table, but there will come a day. There are some principles that are simpler to understand. Actually, they're easier to understand than to practice."

"What are those, Dad?" Marcus asked.

"They have to do with conduct. As men, we have a great responsibility. As businessmen, it is even greater because our actions affect more people. It was important to your grandfather that he pass those character traits to me, and it is important that I pass them on to you."

Having pricked his interest, Tomas inquired, "Just what are these things, Dad?"

"Well, one of the characteristics is honesty. By that, I mean being sincere, truthful, trustworthy, honorable, fair, and genuine. Doing what is right even when no one is watching. Of course, this means that whether you are dealing with employees, suppliers, friends, or family, all must be treated with the same set of principles to keep from making mistakes."

"Dad," Tomas asked, "how do we keep from making mistakes?"

"By making good decisions," Zachary responded.

Marcus quickly asked, "But how do we make good decisions?"

Zachary leaned back in his chair and, with a twinkle in his eye, simply said, "By making mistakes!"

Marcus and Tomas looked across the table at each other, amazed by their dad's wisdom. Tomas turned to his dad and said, "I feel like you just dumped a huge weight on us. How on earth are we to learn all this?"

Understanding the enormity of his words, Zachary simply responded, "Practice!" Then he added, "I have been including both you boys in the workings and growth of this business since you were little. I have given both of you tasks to see how you handle the responsibility. Your jobs are providing the practical experience required to make good decisions. Remember this, there will always be a temptation to cut corners, to go for the quick buck. However, I've learned the quick buck always costs the most in the end."

Zachary sat back in his chair, took a sip of his coffee, and allowed his sons a moment to absorb all that had been said. Then he began to cast a vision for the future. "I see you boys as a team much like the partnership forged between your grandfather Masses and myself. Each of you has shown promise in the areas to which you have been assigned. Marcus, your suggestions on streamlining our assembly have been noted. If you continue to exercise good judgment, it would be my expectation that someday you will assume the role of company president. Tomas, set your sights on replacing Howard Tryggestad. When you get the opportunity to lead the sales team, lead them to excellence as he has done and give your brother the challenge of filling an ever-increasing demand. By the way, Tomas, your ideas about computerizing inventory control have begun to be implemented. Good work, son. That was a great idea."

Zachary pushed his chair back and said, "Well, that's enough business talk today. Let's take the Lord's advice and use this day for some rest."

Becca, who had been quiet throughout the meal, interjected, "Why I should think so? You men and business, business, business seems like that's all you can talk about."

Zachary just smiled, leaned over, kissed his wife on the forehead, and said, "A very good dinner, Becca."

Before leaving the table, Marcus asked, "Dad, some high school friends are going fishing next Friday and asked me to go along. Could I take the day off?"

"You ask your boss. I don't want you going around George for special favors."

"Okay, Dad, thanks."

Tomas sat quietly in his chair as Zachary and Marcus left the room. Becca returned from the kitchen to remove the rest of the Sunday dishes and noticed Tomas staring blankly ahead.

"Tomas," she said, "is something bothering you?"

Tomas jerked his head from the trance he was in and replied, "Uh, huh, oh I . . . I guess I'm shocked a bit."

"Over what?"

He explained in exasperation his dad's vision for Marcus as company president and how it pigeonholed him as his brother's employee without any chance for consideration."

Becca leaned over, put her arm around Tomas, turned his head so he was looking straight into her eyes, and stated with definite authority, "Listen, son, have patience. These things have a way of working themselves out."

CHAPTER 3

Workday

THE WEEK FOLLOWING Marcus' episode in the Barron County Jail, the Zurbriggen twins were with their father on the way to work. Zachary insisted that his boys arrive at work before the other employees. Marcus, however, objected to be forced into a longer workday than the other employees. "Dad, we aren't management. Why do we have to be there so early?"

Patiently, Zachary explained, "No, you aren't the bosses. You are something much more important than bosses. You are examples! Someday, hopefully, you will be bosses, and I never want it said that my boys didn't earn their way to their positions. Working all the various jobs, as you have done, will give you appreciation for each task when you direct someone else to do it. It will also provide you with the experience to know how long it should take and if it was done properly.

Tomas sat half awake in the backseat, gazing out the window at the countryside along Highway 29 as the car sped along toward Chippewa Falls. They passed Bateman, a wide spot in the road that had a store and a couple of taverns. One of the taverns was a supper club whose façade was fashioned to look like an ocean liner. Soon they were passing Lake Wissota, a man-made lake. Zachary used to tell his boys that for years after the river valley was flooded, entire farmsteads were visible below the water, standing like a community under glass. As they rounded the curve leading over the Chippewa River Bridge, Tomas thought of the tale their neighbor told of seeing a body face down in the river, slowly floating toward the dam. Just the thought gave him the creeps.

Then the Leather Werks plant came into view. It was in a building just on the other side of the river. Masses and Zachary purchased it from the Moscowitz family, who had operated a salvage yard from that location. As they pulled up to the gate, Gus, the night watchman, tipped his hat and fiddled with a ring of keys while struggling with Radar, the overly exuberant watchdog. Radar had come with the building. It was the only home he had ever known. The Moscowitz's said he was better protection than the entire police force.

George Renner was the second car entering the parking lot that morning. Marcus waited for George to get out of the car, and they walked together to the production office. Both boys had worked in assembly, maintenance, and shipping while they were in high school. Now that they were in college, Zachary was introducing them to the business side of the company. George was one of the first hires when the business started to grow. He, like Howard Tryggestad in sales, was fiercely loyal to the Zurbriggens. George was a no-nonsense man. Things were pretty much black and white in his thinking. He was a stout fellow, not too heavy, but of good size. He had a thick head of hair that even in his mid-fifties had not grayed. George was even tempered and fair. His presence commanded respect, and all those around him gave it to him. His stern gaze gave the impression that he was always in thought, and his methodical gum chewing supported that image.

"What are we doing today?" Marcus asked as they made their way to the building.

"Reorganize two of the lines," he responded. "They've got bottlenecks that's slowing down production. Then we have to familiarize ourselves with the new computer sheets those machines are spitting out. We still have to maintain our physical inventory method while converting over to the computerized methods just to make sure things are accurate.

"Isn't that just doubling our work?" Marcus grumbled.

George gave Marcus a questioning gaze then answered, "I suppose so, for now, but I hear these computers are the coming thing."

"Leave it to my brother to find a way to make us work harder. I wish Dad hadn't listened to him. What sense does it make for the sales department to set the production schedule? They know nothing about the physical production of our product.

George looked down at his desk, not to study anything but to exercise the patience he was known for, and then he said, "Marcus, you know it isn't that way at all. All the managers meet and discuss our individual problems and needs. We set goals and decide together how to achieve them."

"Ya right!" Marcus mumbled.

*   *   *

Tomas arrived at the sales office and began listing the calls that he and Howard were going to make during the week. Howard Tryggestad was a short, round little man whose remaining hair was cut flat on top. His attire was beyond conservative, some would say stodgy, and he walked with a slight limp from a bout with polio when he was a youngster. He was not at all one would picture as a vice president, but Zachary knew the customers trusted him implicitly, and his work ethic trumped any fancy-suited sharpie in the business.

Howard arrived, carrying a large well-worn briefcase under his arm. "Good morning to ya, Tomas," he greeted. "Have a good weekend?"

"Actually, I had a strong end," Tomas smugly replied.

Howard gave him a puzzled glance.

Tomas laughed and said, "Well, isn't that better than a weak end?"

Howard, being serious minded, shook his head over the wise crack and began greeting other salesmen as they arrived.

Precisely at eight o'clock, Howard brought the meeting to order. "Gentlemen, as all of you are aware, there is just one month remaining to top off your totals for your summer bonuses. Well, I have some good news that will enhance your rewards quite nicely. Mr. Zurbriggen has put his stamp of approval on discounting certain items that will be sure to increase your sales numbers." He handed some papers to a salesman in the front row and motioned for him to pass them out. "Here is a list of discounted items," he began. "Most of them are overstocked inventory, and it would be good to move them out before the fall production begins. Look at the handout you just received, and notice the sale incentives you can offer your customers for the next month." He then began to emphasize the benefits to both the customer and to the salesmen.

"First, with any order your customers place that is 25 percent over their last year's monthly average, you can offer them 50 percent off the regular wholesale price on the discounted merchandise. Or if a customer does not place an order 25 percent over their last year's average, you may offer them any of the discounted items for 30 percent off.

"These are the steepest discounts we have ever offered. I suggest you use them to help your customer's bottom line and, of course, enhance your own bonuses. Now remember my advice as you head out. Call ahead for an appointment, even to potential customers. Courtesy is our trademark. Cold call only if absolutely necessary. Always take your samples in the store to show the customer even if they're familiar with the product. Feeling that fine leather in their hands at 30-50 percent off is enticing. And call me for support even if it is to brag about how big an order you just wrote. I am as near as the phone. Any questions?"

The salesmen were all smiles, but there were no questions, so Howard said, "Let's pray."

Howard made a practice of leading the men in prayer each time he sent them out on the road. He prayed for their safety, for the well-being of their families, mentioning each wife and child by name. He also prayed for their customers and for their success. It was no wonder he had their respect even from those who didn't include calling on God as one of their priorities.

CHAPTER 4

Transition

IT WAS FRIDAY afternoon. George Renner and Howard Tryggestad were heading back to Chippewa Falls after spending the day at a production and sales seminar in Wausau Wisconsin. The two men had been employed at Zurbriggen's since its early expansion and had become good friends. They causally chatted about the day's events as they approached the outskirts of Abbotsford.

"They sure throw a lot of hype into their presentations," George commented.

"Yep, they sure do," Howard replied, "but it's necessary. Look at it this way. By the time they deliver their message to us, then we take it and try to motivate our managers, then they take it and try to motivate the workers. It gets watered down four times by people who don't have the same talent for presenting like the seminar folk do."

"Ya, I guess you're right," George agreed. "I never thought of it that way. Whoa . . . Looks like we're going to have to wait for a train," he said as he pointed to the railroad signal gates lowering and warning lights that started to flash ahead of them. George slowed and came to a stop a few feet away from the gate. They continued their discussion as the freight train came rattling across the intersection.

A block away, Harvey Liddell was returning to the coop from making rural gas deliveries. As he approached the rail crossing, he began to apply the brakes of his two-ton truck. He let out a surprised gasp when the brake pedal plunged to the floor. He tried to downshift, but the split second between the brake failure and his attempt to slow the truck proved futile. His truck lunged forward and rammed into the rear of a brown Chevy stopped at the railway crossing.

As the car made contact with the train, it spun sideways, which, if it had not been for the truck's momentum, could have ended the encounter as a bad accident. However, the gas truck continued forward, smashing broadside into the car and driving it beneath the wheels of the train. A shower of sparks shot out from beneath the train amid the screeching train wheels and the crunching and mangling of metal against metal. The crash sent out horrific sounds so ghastly they sucked one's breath away.

Before the engineer could stop, the little Chevy had been rolled and compacted into a ball of mangled steel, and the lives of two fine gentlemen passed from reminiscing about a sales seminar to standing before their creator.

*   *   *

Zachary had just returned home from work and was relaxing in his favorite chair, watching birds playfully fluttering about the bird feeder outside his den window when the phone rang.

"Hello."

"Is this Zachary Zurbriggen?" the voice at the other end asked.

"Yes, it is. Who is this speaking?"

"Mr. Zurbriggen, this is the chief of police in Abbotsford. Sir, I have a bit of bad news."

"My goodness, Chief, what is it?" Zachary responded by sitting erect in his chair, expecting it to be concerning one of his boys.

"There has been an accident here in Abbotsford. Sir, two of your employees have been killed!"

"What? Killed! Who? How?"

"The identification that we retrieved listed them as George Renner and Howard Tryggestad. I'm terribly sorry, Mr. Zurbriggen. I just got off the line with the gentlemen's wives, and they both asked me to call you."

"Oh my, I don't know, I mean, what happened?"

"It was a car, truck, and train collision, sir. The details will be forthcoming."

"Chief, do you know where Mrs. Renner and Mrs. Tryggestad are now?"

"They were at home a few minutes ago when I talked to them."

"Okay, thank . . . thank you, Chief, goodbye."

Zachary hung up the phone and sat back in his chair, stunned from the news. Gathering his thoughts, he yelled, "Becca, come quick. Come, we must go!"

Becca, noticing the urgency in Zachary's voice, came quickly from the kitchen. "What is it, Zachary?"

"Come, there has been an accident. We must go."

Fear spread over Becca's face as she, like Zachary, suspected it was concerning their sons. Zachary pulled the car out the driveway, leaving a shower of gravel spray behind him. It wasn't until he was on Highway 29 headed for Chippewa that Becca got a word out of him.

"We have to go to the Renners and the Tryggestads," he began to explain. "George and Howard have been killed."

Her face suddenly contorted as she asked, "What happened, Zachary?"

"I don't know much. That was the police chief from Abbortsford on the phone. All he said was there was an accident with a train. That's all I know."

"Oh, our poor friends. How terrible. Do Myrna and Rosemary know?"

"Yes. The police chief said he had just talked with them."

"My, oh my, our dear friends. What can we do?"

"Whatever God directs us to do, Becca. Whatever seems right."

*   *   *

Zachary turned off the highway on the east side of town. We'll stop at Renners first," he explained. "Their place is closest."

He turned down the street where George lived and pulled up to a white two-story house adorned with green shutters and flower boxes under the front windows. Memories of the many times they spent together flooded his mind as he pictured George tending the flowers and shrubs next to the walkway and giving a friendly wave as they arrived. He thought of the many birthday parties, the New Years Eve gatherings, and the barbecues in the backyard. They were all gone now. His friend was gone. He felt crushed, but he had to be strong. This was not about him.

"Zachary, come," coaxed his wife, who was already standing on the sidewalk.

He shook his head, hoping to remove the numbness that had overtaken his mind, and exited the car.

Halfway up the walk, the front door opened, and two women, eyes red from crying and holding handkerchiefs over their noses, appeared. Myrna Tryggestad had driven over to the Renners as soon as she received the phone call.

Becca raised her arms and ran to her friends. "Myrna, Rosemary! I'm so sorry."

The three women stood on the sidewalk, hugging and crying, while Zachary stood helplessly at their side. After several minutes, they released their hugs and looked toward Zachary. He said nothing. He just raised his arms in support, first with Myrna, then with Rosemary.

Rosemary said, "Why, Zach, why?"

Zachary looked each of the ladies in the eye and said, "My good friends, I do not have the answer to why. I only know what we are to do and that is for Becca and me to stand with you. Let's go inside."

*   *   *

The ride to work was a quiet one Monday morning. Zachary, Marcus, and Tomas rode down Highway 29 in complete silence. The boys could only imagine the anguish within their father. Only one who had experienced such a deep loss could understand. As they pulled through the company entrance, Gus, the night watchman, tipped his hat in a most solemn manner. Even Radar at his side appeared uncharacteristically subdued. Zachary pulled the car into his parking place and slowly opened the door. Once outside, he paused to stretch his lanky frame, hoping to work out some of the aches that continued to linger. He looked toward his sons and said, "Follow me."

They walked to the assembly floor and over to the platform where the managers hung the orders being processed. It was slightly before seven o'clock. Normally, the machines would be humming and warming up for the day's activity. Today all was quiet. Workers stood silently by their machines, and each foreman nodded as the Zurbriggens walked by.

Zachary took a position on the platform with a son on either side. He cleared his throat and began, "My fellow workers," his voice cracked, and he paused to regain composure. "Today is one of those days in life for which we are never adequately prepared. Today is a day that makes life *gut-wrenchingly* hard. Today, for the rest of us, begins the first day of the rest of our lives without two quality partners that gave their heart and soul to making things better for you and for me. I know what my friend, George Renner, would say. He would say, 'Enough already, I'm exactly where I have been planning to go, home with my Savior Jesus.' And with that special twinkle in his eye, he would continue, 'It's too bad about the rest of you. You still have to wait awhile.'

"Well, that's what George would say, but here's what I have to say. I'm hurting. I'm hurting for my loss, for George's family's loss, and for your loss. Ya know, he loved all of you. He may not have told you so with his words, but think about how he handled things here. He did it with tender, loving care, not just for a product, but for each of you and for each customer. We can honor George by upholding his values. For now we need to honor his family. You can do that by attending the funeral Wednesday morning. It will be a dual ceremony for both George and Howard. Because a large turnout is expected, it will be held in the high school gymnasium. The Leather Werks will be closed Wednesday out of respect for George and Howard. I encourage each of you to attend. It will be a day off work with full pay. Thank you."

As Zachary turned away, one hand clap started, then two, and then the entire floor resounded with a slow, methodical applause of appreciation. Zachary gave a nervous nod toward the employees, turned and motioned for the managers to gather around. "Gentlemen," he started, "it is obvious that we are in a difficult situation. It is also obvious that we have a heavy responsibility. We must step up and continue." He put his arm around his son's shoulder and said, "It also was apparent to you that my son Marcus was being groomed to take George's position. Here is where I am going to ask for your cooperation. Marcus is young. He needs experience, but for the long-term benefit of the company and all these jobs, we must have a smooth transition. It is my request that you help in that transition. Do not be afraid to give advice, but if you will, do not begrudge Marcus if he does not always follow it. Even more important, when he falls on his face, help him back up."

The floor managers shook their heads affirmatively and said, "You can count on us, Mr. Zurbriggen."

Zachary motioned for Tomas to follow, and they left the assembly floor and proceeded to the sales office. There, a much smaller group had assembled, but Zachary gave a similar speech leaving Tomas in charge.

*   *   *

The day after the funeral, Zachary summoned Marcus and Tomas to his office. When they arrived, their father was standing and gazing out of his office window, his hands clasped together behind his back. The boys entered and took a seat in front of

Zachary's desk. After several moments without acknowledging their presence, Marcus said, "Dad, you sent for us?"

Zachary slowly turned and faced his sons. "Yes, I did. There is much to be discussed. This week has spun my emotions like a whirlwind, but it also caused me to do some serious thinking. I didn't reveal my plans previously to you boys, but your mother and I had decided that I would retire next year."

"Retire?" Tomas blurted out. "But who would take your place?"

"That's what has caused me to ponder the situation. I have made no secret about how I envisioned the succession to evolve. However, the death of my friends has escalated the time frame. Consequently, Marcus, I want you to recommend one of your foreman to take your position, and I want you to start training to step into my shoes."

Marcus's eyes nearly shot out of his head. "Really," he exclaimed. "Man, this is sudden. I never thought, I mean, it's so quick, I . . ."

"Excuse me," Tomas interrupted. "Dad, may I interject something here?"

"Certainly, son, what it is?"

"A few years ago, Marc and I had a serious discussion about the day when succession became an issue." As he was talking, he opened his briefcase and pulled out an envelope and handed it to his father.

Zachary appeared confused by Tomas's statement, but he took the envelope, opened it and began to read the statement Marcus had signed a few years before. Suddenly, Marcus became aware of what Tomas was doing. His face turned crimson as he jumped up and lashed out saying, "Don't pay any attention to that, Dad. It's a piece of trash! It has no meaning!"

Shocked at Marcus's outburst, Zachary said, "Sit down, boy, and loosen your suspenders. I believe they may be a might too tight." As Zachary continued to read, his eyebrows began to rise above his glasses. When he finished, he looked at Marcus and asked, "Son, what is the meaning of this? Can you give me an explanation?"

Marcus, never having been one for long-range planning, had nearly forgot about his youthful immature indiscretion. "This is, ah, that was years ago," he stuttered. "It was just a brotherly prank."

Zachary, looking quite concerned, asked, "Suppose you explain this brotherly prank because it seems that your brother has taken it quite seriously."

Marcus, suddenly trapped between his past actions and reality, uttered, "I got into a jam while on a fishing trip, and Tom bailed me out. He came up with this cockamamie way I could pay him back. I never thought . . . I mean, it wasn't worth the time he took to write it."

Zachary, not wishing for more details, stood, walked over, and gazed out his window. After a short while, he said, "That about sums it up, Marcus, you never thought."

"Dad," Tomas started to interject, but his father held up his hand for silence.

The minutes slowly dragged by as Marcus and Tomas sat without saying a word and only occasionally stealing a glance at one another. Finally, Zachary turned and faced his sons. "Marcus, I have long appreciated your love of nature and your prowess in the great outdoors. However, I believe I have let it unduly influence me to believe that those attributes could be transferred into effective leadership. What this company requires is someone at the helm who has compassion, strength, and vision to not only grow the company, but to care for all those who contributed to its growth. Son, it is with my deepest regret that I must redirect my desire to place you in the presidency, for although this letter highlights your immaturity, it also shines brightly on a character flaw. No one with a smidgen of common sense would put his John Henry to a piece of paper like that, and for a measly two hundred and forty dollars, really?"

"Dad, surely you wouldn't pass judgment on me for one error and one made long ago."

"No, I wouldn't, Marcus, if it hadn't opened my eyes to other infractions throughout the years that I've ignored. You have, because of circumstances, been thrust into a role with heavy responsibilities. George Renner was a man that will not be easy to follow. I am going to leave you in his position. See to it that you live up to the challenge his mentoring has presented to you. As for you, Tomas, it is very difficult to ignore the foresight you used in what Marcus termed a 'brotherly prank,' albeit cunningly manipulative. My decision is as follows – you will immediately begin to plan for a successor as head of sales. During the next year, you will train this person in the rudiments of the job and in our business philosophy. You will also make yourself available to me so that I may teach you how to lead this organization. Now listen to me very carefully. If at the end of one year I feel I can turn the reins over to you, I will retire. However, if you fail in properly training a new VP of sales and I do not feel you are capable of directing the company, you will be fired, and I will seek a replacement elsewhere." Zachary looked directly into Tomas's eyes, then into Marcus's and said, "Am I understood?"

Both men responded with, "Yes, sir."

"Good," Zachary said quietly. "Now get back to work. You have plenty of it to do!"

CHAPTER 5

Retribution

THE FOLLOWING MORNING, Zachary and his two sons strode across the parking lot and, instead of going to their respective offices, went directly to the sales department. Monday morning was a normal gathering time for the salesmen. Howard used it to start the week off on the right foot, as he put it. The salesmen were casually lingering about, some getting a cup of coffee, some debating the merits of their favorite team's latest trade, others idly doodling on a piece of paper. When the door opened and Zachary entered the room, there was an immediate change in the atmosphere.

"Good morning, gentlemen," greeted Zachary.
"Good morning, Mr. Zurbriggen," they said in unison.
Zachary walked to the front of the room and motioned for his sons to take a seat in the front row. He slowly looked over the gathering of his sales force as their shuffling dissolved into silence as he began, "It's been quite a roller coaster ride, hasn't it, men?"
They nodded and murmured affirmatively.
"Well, hold on, we're going to speed it up!" he exclaimed.

Frowns and looks of bewilderment flooded the room.

Zachary began by explaining his desire to retire. He continued with an explanation of who was to be in charge of the various departments and that Marcus was taking over George Renner's position. It was common knowledge that Marcus and Tomas were being groomed for management positions; however, the news of Zachary's retirement came as a shock. This begged for an answer as to who would lead the company. Anticipating the obvious, Zachary announced that Tomas would begin training as his replacement. Announcing Tomas as Zachary's replacement left them stunned, for Tomas had just assumed Howard Tryggestad's position. One salesman remained quietly in his seat as the rest looked around and wondered what was going to happen next. Prior to the sales meeting, this particular salesman had met with Tomas and was offered the position of sales manager in training, which, if performed successfully, could lead to becoming the next vice president of sales. Zachary allowed an appropriate amount of time to pass for questions to form in the salesmen's minds before he said, "And we have chosen someone from among you to lead our sales group." Suspense filled the room as Zachary said, "Join me in welcoming Joe Moravec as our new sales manager. Joe, please join us up here." Joe stepped to the front amid thunderous applause, evidently indicating he was a popular choice.

*   *   *

In the weeks following the new assignment of roles, Tomas divided his time between sales and shadowing his father. As he grew more confident in Joe's performance, he assumed a greater role in guiding the company. As months passed, the transition appeared to be going smoothly. His former peers readily accepted Joe as their leader, and he proved to be a capable motivator. He was not a Howard Tryggestad, but then, no one could ever be. Good news presented itself when the quarterly sales report came out. It showed that sales were above the previous year.

Later in the year, as the company was gearing up for the seasonal increase, problems started appearing. Customer complaints were increasing, some from old reliable customers who personally knew Zachary. There were complaints concerning missed delivery dates, shipping and billing errors, and an overall dissatisfaction with the Leather Werks customer service. When the customer service department brought this to Tomas's attention, he took each complaint and traced it to its source. And in 99 percent of the cases, it led back to the production floor. Eager to remedy to the situation, Tomas called Marcus to his office to discuss his findings and hopefully arrive at a solution.

Marcus entered Tomas's office swinging his arms and looking around at the domain he considered stolen from him. "You summoned your eminence?"

Ignoring the insult, Tomas said, "Yes, Marc. I need your advice about something. Join me over at the conference table."

"My advice. I thought you could control everything."

"Very funny!" Tomas said, pulling out a chair next to a stack of complaints. "Marc, we have a problem that has been developing with some of our customers." He pushed the complaints over to Marcus and said, "We have served most of these people for many years with only praise from them. Suddenly, we are besieged with complaints."

Marcus thumbed through a few of the complaints, threw the rest on the table, and in a nonchalant manner said, "Don't be concerned about a few grumpy old men."

"A few grumpy old men. Marc, these are some of our best customers. I have followed each of these complaints to their source, and the mistakes are being made in labeling, shipping, and the production floor. All these areas are under your control."

"What is this now, the blame game? What do you expect with increased volume? We have the same number of people and machines pushing out 50 percent more work."

"So what is the answer? Do we need another line?"

"No, this is only a temporary spike. When we get past the seasonal demand, we'll be just fine," Marcus snapped and, without another word, left the office, leaving Tomas confused and unconvinced.

* * *

Becca finished folding clothes from the drier and was delivering them to the bedrooms. As she approached Marcus's room, she overheard him talking on the phone with a girl that he was dating.

"It shouldn't be long now, babe. When Dad gets wind of all the order screw-ups from the customers, Tomas will be history.

"What? Oh, it'll only take a few more slowdowns and order mistakes. We've got a good reputation. It shouldn't hurt the company too much. When I get control, I'll ride in like a white knight and correct things. I may even look like a hero for saving the company."

Becca put her hand over her mouth in disbelief. She nearly dropped the laundry basket as she listened to the devious plot Marcus was forming to oust her Tomas. It was unfathomable that one of her sons would actually put their company in jeopardy because of jealously. She quickly went to her room, trying to calm herself and subdue the ache that was welling up within her. *What should I do? What should I do?* kept going through her mind. *Should I go to Zachary? After all, this rivalry could ruin our business.* Finally in tears, she knelt before her bed and cried out to God for help. After a time of prayer, she dried her eyes with a tissue and glanced in the mirror to straighten her hair, before going downstairs to make a phone call.

* * *

Tomas had converted a portion of his bedroom to a home office. He was at his desk, going over delivery reports that had been found in error, when his mother entered.

"Tomas, we have to talk!" Becca said with firmness.

After relating what she had overheard from Marcus's phone conversation, she said, "Tomas, your brother is the one behind the complaints from customers. He is carrying a grudge from that ordeal years ago in Barron County."

Tomas found it hard to believe that his brother would put the company at risk to get revenge against him. "Marc may be shortsighted," he said, "but he wouldn't go this far. It doesn't make sense. I can't believe it."

"Believe it, Tomas! I can tell by his tone. He will not stop until he has pushed you out."

"What am I to do, Mom? If I stay and fight, it could bring down the whole company. Even if I win, it could destroy the culture Grandpa and Dad created."

Becca took hold of Tomas's arms and looked straight into his eyes. "I'll tell you what you have to do, Tomas, you have to leave!"

"How can I do that? I can't just walk away and leave everything. Even if Marc took over, my bet is that he would run it in the ground within a year. He has never taken the initiative to learn or to think. He wants to lead something without any vision. It would be like the blind leading the blind!"

"I have thought this through, Tomas. Now listen, I have a plan. First, your father doesn't have to retire on the timeline originally set up. He can mentor Marcus until comfortable with his capability. Second, I called my brother Gustave. He is willing to give you something to do until you have time to sort out your next move."

"Oh, Mom, that's like charity. I don't want to be beholden to Uncle Gus."

"Listen to me, Tomas. I know this is against your nature. I know that everything in you wants to stay and fight, but you are not going to. Do you hear me? I love you, and I know best. There are times when you must lose the battle to win the war. This, Tomas, is one of those times! Now we must go tell your father what a great need your Uncle Gustave has for your help."

CHAPTER 6

The Decision

ZACHARY WAS IN his study, fully engrossed in a Zane Grey novel, when Becca and Tomas entered. He loved Zane Grey's books for their exciting portrayal of the Old West. Zachary often mentioned that he felt part of the adventure when reading Zane's books.

"Zach," Becca began, "could Tomas and I have a word?"

Zachary pushed out his lips momentarily, fighting back the urge to say no, especially when he was at a thrilling part of the story. However, being gracious by nature, he laid his book down and waved them in.

"Zach, dear, my brother Gustave called and is in a difficult situation with his business," she lied. "He claims he's so close to the problems, it's like he can't see the forest for the trees. He is asking for is a fresh pair of eyes. Someone who has the ability to see past the problems and enough energy to work out a solution."

"I'm not sure I understand, Becca. Exactly what is he asking?"

"He's asking for Tomas. He's asking that Tomas could come and help."

Zachary stiffened in his chair at that request, and then replied, "Well, it just isn't possible. Tomas is in the process of taking over our business."

"I know that, dear, but you were originally going to have Marcus take your position. Why can't you go back to your original plan?"

The crevices in Zachary's face deepened over that suggestion. "Disruption! It seems that's all I have of late is disruption! Is the Lord against an old man slowing down? I know Marcus was the original choice, but Tomas is doing a bang-up job. I'm not as confident in Marcus." There was a long silence before Zachary asked, "What do you say about this, Tomas?"

Tomas hesitated, scratched his ear, not wanting to lie to his father, and said, "Well, Dad, it isn't my first choice."

"Zach, honey," Becca quickly interrupted, trying to save Tomas from incriminating himself, "At his age, my brother is probably having the same thoughts as you, growing older, saddled with problems, but in his case, he hasn't been able to find a solution."

Zachary winced at Becca's comment. She hit him right in the heart with her logic. In frustration, he muttered, "I don't appreciate getting hit with major decisions like this on such short notice. When would you plan on leaving, Tomas?"

Becca intervened again and said, "He needs help now Zachary, before it's too late."

"Dad, if I have your permission, I'll leave this afternoon."

Zachary shook his head as he pondered yet another transformation. "I guess where's there's a family in need, we have to do what we can do." Zachary regained his composure, reached out for his son, and said, "Let me pray for you, Tomas, before you go."

*   *   *

Tomas packed his car, said goodbye to his mother and dad, and left for Chicago, avoiding any contact with Marcus. The sun was just beginning to set as he approached the small town of Dodgeville in Southern Wisconsin. *"I might as well find a room for the night"*, he thought as a motel sign came into view. After checking in, he asked the clerk if he could recommend a good place to eat.

The clerk said, "I like the Cook's Room up on North Iowa street. It has good food, a hometown atmosphere, and it's not too expensive."

"I'll try it," Tomas said. "Thanks for the tip."

Tomas followed the clerk's directions and spotted the little café by its pink awning hanging over a wooden bench out front. A pot of brightly colored flowers sat next to the bench and on the front window. Cook's Room was neatly painted in gold. The front was a warm, rustic brown tone, giving it a homey appeal. Tomas entered the restaurant and chose one of the brilliantly colored tables close to a glass display case filled with tantalizing desserts.

After consuming a sandwich and a piece of scrumptious strawberry pie topped with three chocolate dipped strawberries, he walked out and noticed a long line of cars slowly making their way down the street. Their speed was slow, allowing Tomas to ask one of the drivers, "Where is everyone going?"

"Down to the Centennial Park," one of them shot back. "The Free Lutheran Church is putting on an outdoor play tonight."

Tomas waved a thank you for the information and thought, *"I have nothing else to do. I might take in some of the local culture."*

The park had an open-air pavilion. Concrete benches were arranged in an arc around the pavilion and were filling up fast. Families had spread blankets out on the grass for their children to use as seating. Tomas, spotting an inconspicuous seat near the rear, quickly sat down. The church had erected a plywood backdrop painted to resemble clouds in the sky. On top they had built a platform large enough to allow four people to stand. A moderator stepped to center stage, and a hush fell over those gathered. "Thank you for coming out," she said. "Tonight we are going to present a portion of Genesis 27 and 28. It is that portion of Jacobs's life where he is fleeing his home in Bethel, fearful that his brother, Esau, will kill him for cheating him out of his birthright. We have entitled our production *Running from Sin*. I hope you enjoy the drama."

The play began with Isaac asking Esau to hunt some venison for him. Then moving to where Rebecca and Jacob were planning to deceive his father. After falsely receiving Isaac's blessing and incurring the wrath of his brother, Jacob flees to his Uncle Laban's home. The play quickly advances to the point where Jacob is a fugitive on his journey and depicts the night where he lays down and uses a stone for a pillow. This depiction caused a deep conviction in Tomas, as he saw the events in Genesis mirror what was happening in his life.

The lights on the pavilion dimmed as Jacob laid his head on the stone to sleep. Moments later, as the pavilion lights were brought back up, a ladder appeared rising to the top of the clouds. On the ladder, angels were going up and down. Suddenly, a flash of light ignited at the top of the clouds as God appeared and delivered his promise to Jacob.

"I am the God of Abraham, and of your father, Isaac. The ground you are lying on is yours! I will give it to you and to your descendants. For you will have descendants as many as dust! They will cover the land from east to west and from north to south; and all the nations of the earth will be blessed through you and your descendants. What's more, I am with you, and will protect you wherever you go, and will bring you back safely to this land; I will be with you constantly until I have finished giving you all I am promising."

Then Jacob woke up, . . . "God lives here!" he exclaimed in terror. Jacob vowed to God: "If you God will help and protect me on this journey and give me food and clothes, and will bring me back safely to my father, then I will choose Jehovah as my God! And this memorial pillar I have built shall be a place of worship; and I will give you back a tenth of everything you give me!"[1]

The play concluded and Reverend Atwood gave a short message, telling those gathered that God loved them and wants to communicate with them today, just as He did to Jacob. He ended by asking, "Would you like to know what God is trying to tell you? If so, remain for a time to chat about it."

---

[1] Taken from the Living Bible translation of Genesis 28:13-22 with some alterations.

The uncanny resemblance to his situation unnerved Tomas. He left the park without speaking to anyone and returned to his motel, feeling strangely upset by Jacob's story. He tossed and turned all night, and sleep was only momentary between bouts of restlessness. Remnants of the way he had cheated his brother and how he had shamed him in front of his father flashed through his dreams. Now Marc's bitterness was escalating to the point of possibly destroying the company, and it was all his doing.

The next morning, he slowly slid his feet to the floor. Leaning his elbows on his knees and burying his face in his hands, he pondered on the things that were occurring in his life. Needing to clear the sleepiness from his head, he stumbled to the bathroom and took a long shower. Afterward, as he sat on the edge of the bed, he noticed a Gideon Bible on the lamp stand. Opening it to Genesis 28:10, he read the account of Jacob and his encounter with God. "Oh, I want that," he cried. "I want that. God, can you help me make sense out of all this? I've gone to church all my life. I know about you. I know about your son, Jesus, but I don't really know you! Jesus, please . . . forgive my sin. Please forgive what I have done to my family. Clean me up and be my Lord just as you did for Jacob. Save me, Jesus! I pray you will heal the rift between my brother and me. Please allow me to go back to my father and mother. Amen.

There was no fanfare. There were no bright lights exploding in the air. There was, however, a heavy burden lifted from Tomas as he continued on his way.

CHAPTER 7

Walk-On Shoe Company[2]

A S TOMAS LEFT Wisconsin and crossed into Illinois, he could sense a change. It was subtle at first, but he felt it. The tranquility of rolling hills with farmers tilling their fields disappeared. In their place, commercial buildings, wider roads with more cars appeared. Instead of a distant farm tractor purring away on the countryside, noise from cars and trucks roared along the double-lane highways. Tomas drove south into Chicago and found Cermak Road; from there he traveled to Roosevelt Road where his uncle's factory was located. He didn't know his uncle very well. Gustave and his family had only visited them on two occasions years ago while they were on vacation. He knew that Uncle Gustave had married a

---

2   As I was writing this chapter, I made up a name for the Gustave's shoe company. Later, I found that there is an actual shoe manufacturer by that name. A family company in **Melbourne, Australia,** is behind the Walk-On brand and has been making shoes for more than thirty years. www.walkonfootwear.com.

widow, adopted her two daughters, and later had two sons. Aside from those brief encounters, the Sorensons were strangers to him.

Tomas checked the piece of paper in his shirt pocket for the street number and soon pulled across the street from a building he thought must be the place. It didn't have the address on it, but it looked like a factory. It had the appearance of several one-story buildings built next to one another. A series of short gable roofs went up and down for two hundred feet or more resembling saw teeth. The walls, constructed of grey brick, were as dingy as the surrounding area. A number of glass block windows dotted the building, and over the sidewalk hung numerous power lines, which only added to the dismal appearance. Tomas walked around the corner, trying to find an entrance, and discovered a large wooden door, weathered with age, set back in a recessed area. Over the door was a tarnished brass sign, which read "OFFICE." Except for a worn path on the concrete, the entrance was caked with debris, giving the indication that it had been a long time since it had seen a broom. Tomas reflected back on his teenage years when he and Marcus were assigned the cleaning of the offices and bathrooms at the Leather Werks, cleaning that was to be done to their father's standards. "Pride in the workplace shows itself in the product," he remembered his dad saying. Tomas could not help wondering if the condition of this entryway was reflected in the quality of shoes produced by the Walk-On Shoe Company.

He opened the door to the sound of several typewriters pecking away. Grey metal desks were bumped against both sides of the faded yellow cinder block walls. Between the desks, there was just enough room for a narrow walkway down the center. The lady at the first desk evidently doubled as a receptionist, for when Tomas asked to speak with Gustave Soderstrom, she gave him a quick glance, returned to her work, and said, "Do you have an appointment?"

"Not exactly, but he is expecting me."

"He's in a meeting," she snapped, chewing vigorously on a wad of gum.

"Well, I'll just have to wait then. I've driven several hundred miles to meet with him."

"What's your name and business? I'll slip him a note."

"Would you tell him that his nephew from Wisconsin is here?"

"Oh, you're a relative? Mr. Soderstrom is busy, but your cousin Elsa is here. Shall I get her for you?"

Tomas briefly stammered, not expecting to be introduced to a cousin so promptly. "Ah, yes, that would be fine," he blurted out.

The lady walked to the back of the room and disappeared down a hallway.

After a few minutes, a young woman strode confidently down the hall with a friendly smile. *Oh my goodness,* Tomas thought, *This couldn't be the little Elsa who visited us. She's gorgeous!*

"Hello, you must be Tomas," she said as she extended her hand to greet him. "I'm Elsa."

"Hello, ah, yes, I'm Tomas," he nervously answered. "I haven't seen you since, since . . ."

"Since I was in pigtails and chased you across the yard screaming, 'Not fair, not fair. I tagged you cheater.'"

Tomas laughed as he remembered their vacation visit and remarked, "Well, you sure aren't in pigtails anymore!" His mind wondered momentarily, *That long golden hair hanging around her shoulders and that dimpled smile. Oh, I bet that smile could say hello in any language. I can't believe this is the same girl!*

"Tomas?"

"Huh? What? Oh, excuse me. My mind kinda wandered there."

"I said my dad is free now. I'll show you the way."

"Okay, uh, thanks," he muttered, trying to be as calm as possible.

Elsa led him down several halls to a door with "President" painted on the opaque glass window. She opened the door, and a short balding man wearing a white shirt and suspenders jumped up from behind his desk and said, "Tomas, my sister's boy. How are you?"

"I'm fine, sir. How are you, Uncle Gustave?"

"Fine, fine, and call me Gus, that's how I'm known."

"Very well, uh, Uncle Gus."

"Oh, aren't you the formal one? That's my sister's upbringing. She always wanted things proper. How is Becca anyway?"

"She's very good, healthy and strong."

"And Zachary, how is he doing?"

"He's good, but wanting very much to retire."

"Good to hear. Listen, I want to hear all about your family, but I have some work to finish. Why don't I have Elsa take you over to the house, and we can talk over dinner tonight?"

"That sounds great. I'll see you later then."

"Elsa, show him the way and see that the guest room is made up, will you, hon?"

"Yes, Daddy. I'll take care of him. See you tonight."

"Yes, goodbye, Uncle. See you at dinner," Tomas said awkwardly backing out of the office.

During dinner, Tomas told Gustave the story surrounding the conflict with his brother. Gustave said, "You're welcome to stay here until you figure out what your next step is going to be. Why don't you come down to the plant tomorrow and see how shoes are made?"

"Thanks, I'd like that!"

*   *   *

Tomas ate breakfast with his uncle and rode with him to the plant, as Gustave called it. When they arrived, Gustave introduced him to his foremen, two of which were his sons, and gave them instructions to show him the ropes. Tomas spent the entire day following and listening and asking questions. What he learned from the foremen amounted to excuses for how poor they were doing.

"The foreign imports were crushing American shoe manufacturers," Gustave's oldest son, Mikkel, said.

Nicolai, his younger brother chimed in, "There were no good workers anymore. We try to push these lazy dogs, but they only have one speed – *slow!* You would think they would want to protect their jobs and turn out more production, but the mush heads can't think that far.

The next day, Tomas asked the head foreman, Ace McConnell, if he could work on the lines.

Ace replied, "Sure, maybe you can show these slackers a thing or two."

For the next week, Tomas went from one assembly operation to the next, all the while trying to mix with the workers. He worked next to them, he took breaks with them, he ate lunch with them; but most of them thought he was a management spy sent to check up on their work, and they resented his presence.

The second week, Tomas received permission from his Uncle Gus to organize the maintenance staff into cleanup crews. They started by cleaning and painting in the break room. After it was put into tip-top condition, Tomas set up a daily cleaning schedule to make sure it stayed that way. The next project was the factory, which proved to be more challenging. Beginning with washing the light fixtures and cleaning each bulb, they moved on to scrubbing the walls and windows. It most likely was the first time they had ever been cleaned, judging by the filthy black puddles of water pooling on the floor. It was interesting to observe the various reactions to Tomas's efforts. As the work progressed, the workers began to make favorable comments on the improvements. The foremen, on the other hand, grumbled and complained that Gustave had given his nephew too much latitude, and he was wasting time and money. Two of the most vocal were Mikkel and Nicolai. However, Tomas was not deterred. He launched right into painting the factory walls. It took a month to complete, but the result was a factory that looked brighter and smelled cleaner, with a noticeable change in employee morale beginning to show up in small production increases. Go figure!

Again, Tomas approached his Uncle Gustave with other ideas. "Uncle Gus, I would like to continue to clean up the factory and thought the exterior could use a sprucing up as well. Also, I'm sure you know that I have worked on the assembly lines. I have talked to the all foreman and to many of the workers, and I believe there are things that can be done to increase efficiencies. If you agree to give me the authority, I'll begin to implement them."

"Tomas, the improvements that you have made are already showing dividends, but just because you're a relative, I can't let you work for nothing. What kind of a wage do you want if you stay around to do these things?"

"Uncle Gus, if I am to stay and apply what I know," he paused, took a piece of paper from his pocket and wrote down a number, "this is what I earned at the Leather Werks in the sales manager position. However, there is something I would ask in addition to a salary."

"And what might that be?" Gustave asked with upraised eyebrows as he glanced at the number Tomas had written.

"I would like your permission to date Elsa."

With an ever-present awareness of striking a good deal, Gustave replied, "Oh, you would, would you?"

"Yes, sir."

"You do realize that she's your cousin?" Gustave replied, fully aware they were cousins by adoption.

"Yes, I do, but you have heard of kissing cousins, haven't you, Uncle?"

"Now wait just a minute. First, you're talking about a date, now you're talking about kissing. I think you're running a little faster than I travel, young man."

"It's just an expression, Uncle. You know that."

"Well, that aside, I think she may be a bit young for you. You may do better considering Henrika, my older daughter."

"Beg your pardon, Uncle, but I asked about Elsa."

"I know what you asked, Tomas, but you kinda startled me with that big number you wrote. Wouldn't seem right you making more than the company president."

Tomas knew his uncle was blowing smoke, but he played along by saying, "Oh no, sir, that would never do."

"You know, Nephew, Henrika doesn't have a boyfriend right now."

"Very interesting that you bring up that fact at this time. You do know, Uncle, that I don't run a dating service, don't you?"

"Oh, yes, I am aware of that. I just am having a hard time getting that big number out of my mind. You understand, Tomas, sometimes a man is taken by surprise, and it may take a while to adjust after a shock like that."

It was all too obvious where this conversation was going, so Tomas said, "I tell you what, Uncle Gus, you write down a number that includes your blessing to date Elsa, and we'll see if we have a deal."

Gustave sat back down behind his desk amid several grunts and groans, scribbled down a figure, and handed it back to Tomas.

Noticing that is was twenty-five percent less than his number, Tomas puckered his lips and said, "I didn't hear anything from you about Elsa."

Gustave smiled and replied, "Oh, yes, you have my permission. I thought that was understood."

Tomas extended his hand and said, "Uncle, you have just made the best deal of your life. I'm sure you will get a good return."

*   *   *

Tomas and Elsa began dating, but Henrika seemed to find an excuse to be included in whatever they planned. This annoyed Tomas and made private conversation with Elsa nearly impossible. However, as the weeks and months passed, the couple became quite creative in ditching the older sister, mainly because Henrika became bored playing the third wheel. At the same time, Tomas continued to evaluate the workings of the Walk-On Shoe Company. His assessment included the lackluster marketing effort the company was making. With the reluctant approval of Gustave, Tomas contacted and met with Robert (Rob) Buchanan, a classmate of his from UW-Eau Claire. Tomas knew Rob was an up and coming marketer. Immediately out of college, a leading manufacturer of dental products had hired him to work in their marketing department. The two young men had stayed in contact after college, and Tomas remembered Rob commenting about his job. He had said, "These guys make toothbrushes, and if you're going to sell more of 'em, ya gotta find a new way to get them off the shelves. That's where I come in. I think up the gimmicks!" He may have been an upstart, but he was aggressive and positive, with an attitude that nothing, absolutely nothing, could prevent him from reaching his goals.

As a young single man, he immediately spotted an opportunity in the marketplace. He was acutely aware of what a turnoff bad breath was on a date. Normally, most guys would have carried some breath mints, and that would be that. Not Rob. He concocted, developed, and presented to the vice president of his division an idea he called Fresh Mouth. It was a strong mouthwash product dried and embedded onto thin dissolvable strips. The strips were loaded in a dispenser that allowed removal one strip at a time. The flavored strip would dissolve immediately when placed on the tongue, providing an instant blast of freshened breath. In his presentation to his boss, Rob guaranteed this product would remove 90 percent of the odor causing bacteria in the mouth, leaving the user to feel fresher and more confident in any situation. In typical Rob fashion, he boldly moved to prove his claims by calling forth one of the other members of his marketing team who was notorious for having bad breath. He had the man breathe into the vice presidents face, achieving the expected reaction from the VP, and then directed the man to place a Fresh Mouth prototype strip on his tongue. When the man blew into the VP's face the second time, it was with a completely different response. The VP loved the idea, it went into production, and the company sold millions of them. It also placed Rob several notches higher on the corporate ladder.

Rob was already making a salary well above what Tomas was being paid, but through a series of negotiations and the promise of the challenge in a smaller company versus being just one little speck on a corporate giant's wall, they brought him on board. Of course, Uncle Gus managed to include 10 ten percent pay cut in Tomas's wage before he approved the hire.

Rob was not a handsome man. He was full in the face with light sandy hair. Even though his weight was slightly over what would be called healthy, he was extremely energetic and full of fun. He was one of those characters who always thought out of the box, but his highest quality was that he was a man of good character. On the first weekend after he moved to Chicago, Elsa arranged to set him up with Henrika on a double-date. The foursome took in some of the downtown Chicago sites, went to a movie, and ended the evening sipping strong coffee in a small sidewalk café. Everyone had a hilarious time. Rob was so full of stories. Before the night was over, the other three had sore bellies from laughing so hard. Rob was quite enamored with Henrika and vice versa, so this became a regular occurrence.

*   *   *

Rob's enthusiasm lifted all those around him. He motivated the sales staff, implemented bonus and commission programs, and after only nine months, sales were slowly inching upward because of his influence. He and Tomas were a dynamic team, and when they met for strategy sessions, it was as if the room was filled with electricity. During their last session, however, Rob was somewhat subdued.

Tomas asked, "Hey, bro, what's on your mind? You seem rather quiet tonight."

"I'm boxed in."

"What do you mean?"

"Our product. It needs to be redesigned. The overseas competition is ahead of the curve on this, and if we don't retool, we'll be left selling shoes to Grandma."

"Any ideas?"

"Ya, but ole Uncle Gus ain't gonna like it."

"Spit it out."

"The Brown Shoe Company has been able to hold its own against these foreigners. They are always coming up with something innovative."

Tomas sensed more was coming from Rob, so he said, "I know there's something just burning inside you, so spill it already."

"Okay, but Uncle ain't gonna like it."

"Let me handle Uncle Gus. What are you thinking?"

"We need to hire Brown's head designer!"

"Whoa! You're right about one thing. Uncle ain't gonna like it."

"Look, Tomas, if we get someone on our side who can knock down that we've-always-done-it-this-way mentality, we can carve out a market niche and stay profitable."

"I agree, but how do we go about hiring this person?"

"No problem. I have already contacted him. He's flying in tomorrow and will be here about one o'clock."

"You did what? What did you tell him? How am I going to explain this to Uncle Gus?"

THE MAKING OF A MAN

"It's like you just said bro, you can handle Uncle Gus."

*   *   *

At precisely one o'clock, Lowell Bertram arrived at the Walk-On Shoe Company. Tomas, Rob, and Lowell met for three hours. They discussed the world and domestic markets, the future of American-made goods, and what possibilities lay ahead. Lowell was definitely an out-of-the-box thinker as well. He and Rob jelled immediately. During the last half hour of the conversation, the threesome concentrated on the possibility of joining together.

"Why would you consider leaving a successful and enterprising company like Brown?" Tomas asked.

"Good question," Lowell responded. "I've been with Brown for thirty years, and am at a point where I can retire. I don't want to retire, but I can."

"So?" Rob interjected, sensing a way to put this deal together. "Why don't you?"

"Because I love a challenge, and, boys, what I see here at Walk-On is definitely a challenge."

Salesman Rob took over, pulled out a piece of paper, and laid out a plan that gave Lowell a modest but comfortable salary and a percentage of every Bertram-designed shoe sold after all fixed, and variable costs were covered. The men shook hands and Lowell left.

Rob turned to Tomas and said, "Now what do you think of that?"

Tomas scratched the back of his head, pondering an answer, and said, "Unbelievable! How in the devil am I going to sell that to Uncle?"

"Smoothly, Tomas, real smoothly. You can do it. You've done it before you can do it again. I've got confidence in you. Just remember – *smoothly!*" he repeated with a grin a wide as his face.

CHAPTER 8

Two for One

TOMAS SCHEDULED A meeting with his uncle the next day. It was a meeting he dreaded. They met in Gustave's office, and as the two sat down, Tomas began by saying, "Uncle, the improvements we made have increased production on the floor, and Rob's efforts have increased sales, but it's not enough."

Gustave squinted at Tomas and replied, "It seems to me if you cut production costs and increase sales, we must be doing something right."

"It's certainly better than going in the opposite direction, however, the foreign goods are increasing their market share every quarter. Uncle, if that trend continues, you will be out of business in five years."

"Pshaw! Good ole American quality has always beaten those cheap imports."

Tomas countered, "Those cheap imports are just that – *inexpensive* – but their quality continues to improve."

"I know you pretty well by now, Tomas. You didn't come in here to discuss foreign competition. What's on your mind?"

Tomas cleared his throat and replied, "We need a head designer!"

"We have a head designer."

"No, you have a designer whose head is stuck in the fifties! We need innovation, someone who has his eye on the pulse of the buying public."

Gustave began to get a little edgy over the direction this conversation was going, but he asked, "And just where do you propose to find such a person?"

"The Brown Shoe Company. Their head designer is Lowell Bertram."

"Brown? That's a good company. There's no way the head designer from Brown would come here!"

Tomas paused a few seconds before saying, "He'll be here two weeks from tomorrow."

"*What!*" Gustave said, jumping up from his chair. A crimson red crept up his neck and consumed his entire face as he shouted, "What in blazes have you done, Tomas? We can't afford someone from Brown!"

"You can't afford not to, Uncle. Look here," Tomas said as he pulled out the compensation plan he and Rob put together. "He begins with a modest salary and receives an incentive commission only after all expenses are covered and only on the commission of the shoes that he has designed, not on our present lines.

Gustave, growing increasingly irritated, spewed out, "Tomas, this time, you've gone too far. It's too much, I tell you, too much!"

"Uncle Gus, I mean no disrespect. My whole time here, I've only done what I thought would help the company, and it certainly isn't because of the big wages I'm receiving. But you have a decision to make. You can join us in this market battle with the new designer, or you will have to proceed without Rob and me. We do not want to be part of a sinking ship.

Gustave returned to his desk, buried his head in his hands, and said nothing. Tomas realized that his uncle's ego was damaged by his actions, but in his heart, he knew it was in his uncle's best interest.

Finally, Gustave broke the silence and said, "Tomas, you've hurt me deeply. You've backed me in a corner, and I have no way out, but by the bloody blazes you will pay for this! I'm cutting your salary by another fifteen percent. And since you're so enamored with incentives, you can try to make it up by taking the same percentage commission on this Bertram character's designs that you gave him."

Realizing that Uncle Gus saw this as a losing endeavor but believing it as an opportunity, Tomas replied, "Uncle, are you sure that's the way you want to handle this?"

With an angry, disgusted tone, Gustave spit out, "How else can I teach you proper respect for authority? You made a decision without my approval, now you will live with it."

"Yes, sir," Tomas replied, "I will."

*   *   *

Two weeks had passed when a handsome man in his late fifties entered the Walk-On offices, displaying an air of authority he intended to be humorous. "Young lady," he said to the girl at the front desk, "Where is my office?"

"Who are you?" she asked, taken back by a stranger's boldness.

"I'm your head designer!" he announced.

She nervously got up and ran to the back office, seeking help with this odd intruder.

Tomas, seated at his desk, overheard the encounter and stepped out. "Lowell, are you deliberately trying to unnerve everyone? Come on in. I'll introduce you to my uncle."

Lowell gave a hearty laugh, took the hand of the young lady he had alarmed, and said, "A thousand pardons, miss, but I have only one chance to make a first-day impression."

"Well you certainly did that," she uttered, slinking back onto her chair.

Tomas led him back to Gustave's office and knocked on the door. "Come in," he responded.

"Uncle Gus, this is Lowell Bertram. Lowell, Gustave Soderstrom, the owner of the company."

"Mr. Soderstrom, I am very glad to meet you. Over at Brown, we have talked about your company frequently."

"You have, have you? Did they ever talk about it being hijacked?"

"No, sir, but there was a rumor about it being detoured – for the common good I was told."

"Very funny. Do you charge extra for being a comedian?"

Not allowing Gustave's sour attitude to deter him, he said, "Not at all, sir. It's built into the compensation."

Tomas didn't want the sparring to get out of hand, so he suggested they go to the design department.

Orley Ostergren, the head designer, was absorbed in drawings as the three men entered the room. "Orley," Gustave announced, "Tomas has hired this fella to bring new designs into the company."

Orley was shocked and responded, "But . . . but I'm your head designer, Mr. Soderstrom."

"You still are," Gustave tried to assure him. "Tomas went ahead and brought him in to – what was it you said Tomas? To liven up the line?"

"Mr. Soderstom," Orley choked out, "I have been in charge of this department ever since there was a department. Don't you think I should have been consulted in a decision like this?"

"Orley, I'm sorry," Tomas confessed. "This is my doing. Uncle Gus had nothing to do with it."

Orley stiffened, picked up his coat, and said, "Then this is my last day, goodbye!" and quickly left the room, with Gustave shouting, "Wait, Orley, wait! We'll work this out."

Lowell turned to Tomas and said, "This has sure been an exciting morning. I think I will like it here."

*   *   *

Later that day, Gustave called Tomas and Rob to his office. Spreadsheets showing past quarterly reports were spread across his desk. As the two were seated, Gustave pointed to the figures and said, "Gentlemen, month after month, our sales have risen. Month after month, our expenses per item have decreased. What do you make of that?"

"What do you make of it, Uncle?" Tomas shot back.

"I'll tell you what I make of it! Until a few days ago, I would have said we're headed in the right direction. I looked over the pro forma you boys made, and the cost of setting up new lines of product are staggering. It appears to me that for every percent increase in profit that we have made, we will have to invest two percent in capital costs."

Tomas carefully contemplated a response, then replied, "Uncle Gus, didn't it require a capital investment each time you retooled for a new design? And didn't it take time to manufacture, market, and distribute before a return could be expected?"

Gustave said nothing but sent Tomas an ugly scowl.

Tomas continued, "Oh, I get it! You're still sore because we didn't consult you on this hire. That's what makes it hard to say what I have to say!"

Silence filled the room. Gustave was wondering if he had pushed his nephew too far and he was quitting. Rob also was thinking, *What are you doing, bro?*

Tomas interrupted the awkward quiet by saying, "Uncle Gus, will you give me permission to marry Elsa?"

Gustave looked up with a blank expression. He was caught completely off guard. Rob too exhibited surprise. He leaned forward in his chair, his jaw hanging open like a bumbling idiot. Composing himself, he slapped his leg and said, "Well, I'll be darned!"

Gustave recovered enough from the unexpected question to say, "What?"

Tomas repeated, "You heard me, Uncle. Would you give me your blessing to marry Elsa?"

"Wh . . . where is this coming from? One minute we're talking business, and the next, matrimony!"

"This is coming from the heart, Uncle Gus. I was struck by her from the first day I came here."

Still attempting to make the shift in subjects, Gustave sputtered, "Well, what about Henrika? She's older. It would break her heart to see her little sister married out from under her."

Rob piped up, "I can solve that, Uncle Gus. Give permission for me to marry Henrika."

Gustave, looking completely baffled, said again, "What's going on here? Are you two ganging up on me? Are you just trying to throw me off?"

Now it was Tomas's turn to be taken back. He asked, "Rob, are you serious?"

"Never been more serious," Rob said with finality. "We could have a double wedding."

Both men looked over at Gustave and said, "Well?"

CHAPTER 9

"Have You Been 'Z'ed'?"

TOMAS, ROB, AND Lowell put in many late nights, studying footwear demographics, critiquing Lowell's designs, costing out manufacturing operations and materials before deciding on two basic designs. To appeal to the younger, trendy male and female, they called their creation *Coolees – by Walk-On*. For the more sophisticated set, they named their new creation **pro-fessionals** – *by Walk-On*. Neither style would compete with Walk-On's present lines; they would instead broaden the company's appeal.

It took six months of doggedly hard work to prepare these designs for production. It was now time to enter the marketing phase. Uncle Gustave resisted each marketing plan Rob brought forth, adamantly opposing radio and television. Finally, he consented to budget of one hundred thousand dollars, but only if spent on a print campaign. Lowell and Rob pleaded for more, but Gustave stood firm.

Rob, Lowell, and Tomas decided to use the majority of the budget in the Midwest. They felt trying to cover the entire country with such a small budget would dilute the message. It cost twenty-five hundred dollars to purchase names and addresses of potential Midwest stores with the demographic profile they were trying to reach. It cost another thirty-five thousand dollars to print and mail a quality full-color brochure directly to the people in those markets. Twenty-five thousand was allocated to slick-colored magazine ads, ten thousand to newspapers, and the last of the budget was spent creating eye-catching in-store placards with pop-out shelves to hold shoe samples for all stores carrying Walk-On products nationwide. Walk-On salesmen were instructed to place the displays just inside the store entry, so customers would notice Walk-On products before seeing any other display.

As sales of the new product lines grew, so did the traditional lines. Gustave interpreted this as his mainstay products lifting the new lines from obscurity. However, as sales grew, so did Tomas's commissions. In eight months, they made up for half of what Gustave had deducted. A growth trend like that gave Tomas confidence that now he could provide a home for Elsa, and a wedding date was set. Rob the optimist had pushed to set a date the day Gustave gave his blessing but hung to his proposition that it should be a double wedding, and a double wedding it was to be.

Gustave walked the aisle with a daughter on each arm. Both couples recited their vows before God and man and retreated to an elaborate banquet. It was a glorious time. Family and friends from Rob's side and Gustave's side filled the hall. In spite of it being the happiest day of his life, sadness hung in Tomas's heart, for noticeably missing were members of his family, further evidence of the damage created by the conflict with Marcus. In response to the RSVP, the Zurbriggens sent an answer with a simple statement that spoke volumes – "We will be unable to attend. I'm so sorry! Becca"

*   *   *

Tomas and Elsa took a honeymoon cruise to the Caribbean that included several days at an island resort. Late one afternoon, while he sat under a palapa umbrella, gazing at the ocean sunset, an idea burst into his mind, and he began scribbling notes on a scratch pad. The idea so consumed him he could hardly wait to share it with Rob and Lowell. Of course, he was on his honeymoon, so he did contain his excitement until they returned; but on the first day back, he called his two associates to his office and revealed his expansion plan.

"This is a big deal, Tomas," Rob exclaimed, "but I believe the market is right for it. What do you think, Lowell?"

"It's creative, visionary, an exciting concept, but it will cost a bundle. How will you ever get your uncle to go for it?"

"I don't know. I wanted to run it by both of you as a trial run. I'll pitch it to Uncle Gus tomorrow."

Tomas made an appointment with his uncle for the next morning. He was filled with anxiety as he stepped into Gustave's office, knowing his reluctance for change, especially if it cost him money.

"Tomas, my boy, how is the old married man?"

Trying to interject a little humor, Tomas replied, "I don't know, Uncle. How are you?"

Gustave laughed and said, "Oh, you are always with the sharp ones."

Tomas took a seat in front of Gustave's desk and facetiously recounted the honeymoon. "Oh, the romantic strolls on moonlit beaches, the waiters at our constant beck and call, all this with the most beautiful girl in the world. It just made me long for the sound of those machines pounding out shoe after shoe."

"Ya right," Gustave laughed, "but I tell you the sales have continued to remain strong across all the lines. That's very good, huh?"

"That's very good, Uncle," Tomas replied, and sensing an opportunity, he opened with a teaser question. "Uncle Gus, how would you like to make those sales even larger?"

When something pricked Gustave's interest, his ears would quickly move up and down just a little. Tomas noticed their wiggle and proceeded, "You know it does one good to get away from the day-to-day work. While we were gone, I had time to think and plan. I believe I have some very good ideas that will enable us to capture a bigger piece of the market. Would you be interested in hearing them?" Tomas was drawing Gustave in by dangling the bait close, but not so close that he could reach it.

"Of course I want to hear it, but I'll warn you, Tomas, I'm always a bit suspicious when I see your eyes dance like they are right now."

"Uncle, have I ever steered you wrong? Aren't my ideas making you plenty of profit?"

Gustave sat back in his chair, placed his hand on his chin, and said, "Yes, that's true, Tomas, but . . ."

"But what?" Tomas quickly asked.

"Golly, Tomas, you move so fast and furious sometimes you scare the beejeebees out of me, and you know it's the Walk-On name that's keeping those fancy shoes of yours afloat!"

Tomas stood and slowly paced around the room, ignoring Gustave's comment before replying. "I beg to differ with you on that last point, Uncle, and as to fast and furious, what I have in mind cannot be done fast. It will take much study and planning, but if executed properly, it will make you rich."

As Tomas completed that last statement, he noticed Uncle Gus's ears twitch again. "Well let's get on with it," Gustave urged impatiently. "What idea is churning around in that head of yours?"

"Uncle Gus, sit back in your chair and close your eyes. I want you to imagine that all the things I am going to tell you have already taking place. Are you ready?"

"I'm not sure," Gustave answered.

"When you have purged all negative thoughts from your mind, then you're ready. You and I are going to Green Light!"

"Green light. What's that?"

"That's where we think of all the ways we can succeed first, then after we think through what will make an idea succeed. We will critique it and throw out the parts that are unworkable. Can you do that?"

"Tomas, why do I have the feeling that you're conning me?"

"Because you don't understand green lighting. I need you to think positive, to buy in to the idea without rejecting it before you understand it. Remember, afterward, you can throw the whole thing out the door if you don't like it. Okay?"

"I feel a little foolish, but I'll try it."

"Good. I've been studying the under-forty and over-eighteen demographics. This is a group that has money and is willing to spend it. They are also heavily influenced by peer pressure! The youngest of this group want to be considered cool. They want to be different from other groups, but ironically, they become the same as everyone else as they try to be different. Those at the older end find themselves getting closer to forty and want desperately to look younger. That's where we come in!"

Gustave raised one eyelid and said, "How? By making cool shoes?"

"Not just shoes, Uncle. Imagine that Walk-On created a whole new line of products that this group just has to have! I'm talking shirts, pants, scarves, blouses, jewelry, and shorts for both men and women, and yes, of course, shoes. Marketing would entail promotions to create a must-have mentality. We would simply call the products the 'Z'! Our slogan would be 'Have You Been "Z'ed" yet?'" Tomas, in his enthusiasm, had been pacing the floor to deliver the exciting potential of his idea. He stopped, looked over at his uncle, and said, "So what do you think?"

Gustave sat up in his chair, rubbed his hand across his mouth, and asked, "Are we done green-lighting yet?"

"We're done, Uncle. Now we talk about the hurdles to make this work."

"Well, all I got to say is . . . that must have been some honeymoon."

"Oh, it was, Uncle Gus. We had a great time, but I had time to think too."

"I can see that," Gustave replied, "but couldn't you have thought of something practical?"

"I've studied the market, Uncle. It is just as I have stated. Someone is going to recognize this as a gold mine and go after it. I want that someone to be us."

"Tomas, I can't help but admire your enthusiasm and your vision, but we are in the shoe business. You want to go into garments and jewelry too? We don't know anything about that business, and from what I've read, it is very volatile."

"It can be. That is why I propose that we contract out everything except footwear. We will not have to invest in machines, employees, or brick and mortar. Our risk will be contained to our marketing and inventory costs."

"Tomas, I can see how this plan excites you, but I have to tell you, son, I think it's a hair-brained idea. The time and money it would take to launch a project like this would put any businessman in the poor house. No, Tomas, I'm going to red-light this one!"

Tomas lowered his head, not in defeat, but to phrase his response. After a long silence, he said, "Uncle Gus, I feel I have no choice but to follow my gut instincts. I believe this is doable. So I am going ahead with this project on my own. As of this morning, you have my thirty-day notice to leave your employ!"

This caught Gustave off guard. He stammered, trying to collect his thoughts and said, "Nephew, please don't leave me. Don't you think that is a bit hasty? Maybe I have been too hard on you. We can work this out. We have been good for each other. Just last week I had my palm read, and the fortune-teller said that I owe my good fortune to a relative. That's you, Tomas. You must stay. I'll pay you whatever you ask!"

Tomas, shocked and disgusted that his uncle would rely on false spirits such as fortunetellers, replied, "Uncle, you had very little profit before I came. In the beginning, I worked for nothing to clean up your factory. I settled employee grievances. Rob and I developed a marketing plan. We added new designs, and all this increased your wealth tremendously. Yet every time I implemented a plan to increase your business, you lowered my wages. Did you think that was an incentive to keep me here? So I ask you, what about me? How am I to provide for my family?"

"You must stay, Tomas. I'll pay you whatever you ask!"

Tomas thought for a few moments before responding. When he spoke, he said, "Uncle Gus, I don't believe you want me to stay.

You ridiculed and disapproved of everything I tried to do. You were not in favor of bringing Rob and Lowell into the company. At every opportunity, you reminded me that it is your traditional lines that are holding up the lines my staff and I created."

Gustave, grasping the hair at the side of his baldhead, pleaded, "Oh, Tomas, forgive this old man. I know what you say is true, but I was fearful of failure. Please, how can I make it up to you?"

"So you truly want me to stay?"

"Yes, Tomas, you have that – what do they say? – that special touch."

After a long pause, Tomas said, "If you want me to stay, give me ownership of the Coolee and Pro-fessional lines and allow Rob, Lowell, and me the freedom to develop my idea on the side."

Gustave, who had never placed much value on the new brands, eagerly replied, "All right! It will be as you have asked. All I ask is that you will stay with me for six more years."

Tomas replied, "I agree."

That very day, Gustave drew up papers, giving full ownership of the Coolee and Pro-Fessional brands to Tomas and a contract to continue producing them for a 5 percent premium over manufacturing costs.

*   *   *

Tomas organized the start-up by prioritizing tasks. Although they conferred with one another, each person was primarily in the area assigned. Lowell was in charge of design and garment coordination. Rob was to develop the marketing strategy and make contact with the manufacturers. Tomas handled the facility acquisition and arranged financing. Progress was slow since they each had responsibilities with Walk-On. However, Gustave was uncharacteristically cooperative. Tomas suspected it was his uncle's hope that their endeavor would produce more volume for his business. Months passed as the three men labored at selecting basic clothing and jewelry accents designs. Rob created and scrapped several marketing plans, but the most difficult area proved to be financing. Apparently, bankers were of the same mind-set as Gustave for Tomas's presentations all met with an interesting-but-not-right-for-our-portfolio rejection. After his last rejection, a sympathetic banker took him aside and recommended that he contact Park Place Venture Capital in Minneapolis. He explained that they were better suited for a start-up than banks.

Tomas took his advice and immediately made an appointment with their frontline analyst. After three presentations, the last with the CEO and board, they agreed to fund the company with a million-dollar investment package. The funds would be advanced as the company developed a national marketing and distribution plan. In return, PPVC was to receive thirty percent of the net profit for ten years. Tomas walked out of the thirty-story office building, flying so high he felt he could float home without an airplane. That night, he and Elsa dined at Papa's Steak House to celebrate their good fortune. When they returned home, he called Rob and Lowell and gave them an address on Canal Street, with instructions to meet him there at seven in the morning. Both Rob and Lowell pressed him on the outcome in Minneapolis and wanted to know why they were meeting on Canal Street. He only said, "It will be completely clear in the morning."

The next day, Rob and Lowell arrived in front of an abandoned Canal Street warehouse. Lowell said, "This looks like one of those places the mob uses to do away with fellas."

"Maybe Tomas is gonna get rid of us once and for all," Rob mocked.

Lowell pulled on the front door. It opened with a rusty screech as in an Alfred Hitchcock horror movie. Stepping into a musty smelling office, they saw desks that were left where last used but covered with dirt and plaster that had fallen from the ceiling. Lowell was concentrating on cobwebs hanging from light fixture to light fixture when suddenly he was poked in the back with a hard object and a gravely voice said, "Wats ya doin' in here, Bub?" Lowell nearly jumped out of his skin until he turned and saw it was Rob's finger that had stuck him in the ribs.

Disgustedly, he said, "Cut that out," as Rob bent over laughing.

They continued through the office, being careful not to touch any of the filthy surroundings. As they passed one of the private offices, a loud voice sounded behind them, saying, "Good morning." This time, both Lowell and Rob jumped only to see Tomas emerge from the shadows.

"Jeepers Tomas," Lowell said, "Why have you had us come to this creepy place?"

"For a very good reason, gentlemen. This is your new office."

Lowell and Rob gave each other a look, and Lowell said, "Does this mean . . . ?"

And Rob burst out with, "Tomas, you got the money didn't you?"

"A million smackers, boys, and I only had to mortgage my firstborn."

"Holy smackeroos, Tomas," Rob exclaimed. "Where do we start?"

"I've got a crew of temp workers on their way over here. We'll start just the way I started at Walk-On, cleaning and painting. When we have the place presentable, we'll hire designers to take our ideas and tune them up. I want to be ready to hit the fashion scene by next year."

* * *

Together, the three men developed a new brand of shoes, clothing, and jewelry. Classy outfits for every season, each sporting the "Z" trademarks. The jewelry also displayed the "Z." Necklaces had interlocking "Zs." Rings and pins had the letter uniquely fashioned into the design so as not to appear gaudy, but to unashamedly display their signature. Together, with print, radio, and television, they created an image that anybody who is anybody had to be wearing the "Z." On Lowell's suggestion, Rob researched and mimicked the methods used to catapult Buster Brown Shoes into a national company. He hired sixty actors, thirty men and thirty women, and dressed, as Rob liked to put it, "to the Zs!" The teams were given scripts and trained how to present themselves when promoting the "Z" line. They crisscrossed the country, making a splash at every store handling their product. Part of their shtick was to strut their stuff around each town and create attention. TV, radio, and print ads preceded the actors and built anticipation of the upcoming "Z" event. The media was notified when they arrived and the actors made spectacles of themselves. Posing with children, little ole ladies, and, of course, several of their targeted group.

Yes – The "Z" was causing a sensation.

CHAPTER 10

The Right Move

THE "Z" HAD caught on. Rob's marketing plan was so successful the manufacturing and distribution divisions had difficulty keeping up with demand. To satisfy customers, merchants created waiting lists for those wanting items on back order. The first year's sales surpassed all expectations, pleasing everyone, especially the investors at Park Place Capital. Fashion designing required companies to stay on the cutting edge of change, so Tomas hired additional designers to produce creative changes in the next year's product line.

Tomas's business wasn't the only place where productivity was prevalent. During the year, Rob and Henrika had a baby boy. They named him Rueben, and everyone, including the Buchanans, was surprised when in three months, Henrika announced that she was pregnant again. This produced happiness for the couple and sorrow for Elsa, as she became very envious of her sister. Much to the dismay of Tomas, Elsa cried herself to sleep night after night, saddened that she was childless.

"Tomas," Elsa pleaded, "all I ever wanted was to be a wife and a mother. We must have children, we must!"

"Elsa, we have tried," he assured her. "We'll keep on trying. I'm sure the Lord will answer our prayers."

"Let's look into adoption, Tomas. I'm sure there are many children out there who need a good home."

"No, Elsa, we can continue to try on our own!"

When it came to business, Tomas was very decisive. When it came to Elsa, he was a pushover. Within four months, the Zurbriggens were informed that they could adopt two children if they would accept older children rather than newborn. They agreed and adopted Daniel, a four-year-old, and a two-year-old named Nathan.

The rivalry between the sisters intensified as Henrika continued to bear children and Elsa remained barren. It was the fourth year of their marriage when Elsa became aware that her body was changing. A visit to the doctor confirmed her suspicions. That night Tomas arrived home from work to soft music and a candle light dinner. Elsa had taken the boys to their grandparents in preparation for her announcement, and as they sat together, enjoying the quiet ambiance after dinner, Tomas said, "I suppose I will find out eventually, but what do I owe this special treatment?"

Elsa snuggled close to him and asked, "If we could have anything in the world that we want, what would it be?"

Tomas gave her a blank look and was clueless.

"Come on, Tomas, guess," she coaxed.

"Oh, I suppose that the boys grow up to be good and upright."

"Men!" Elsa exclaimed. "You have no imagination."

"Well, what is it that you're trying to draw out of me?"

Elsa stood up, pushed back her hair as if she was to make a very important speech and said, "I'm pregnant!"

Tomas' mouth dropped open as he jumped from the couch shouting, "Really, you're pregnant? For real, you're sure?"

"Yes, I went to the doctor today to confirm it."

"Oh, honey, this is wonderful. See, I told you God would answer our prayers!" Tomas shouted as he lifted her in his arms and swung her around.

"Be careful," she cautioned, "I'm with child, you know!"

God did bless them, and Elsa delivered a nine-pound baby boy, and they named him Joseph.

* * *

The "Z" brand continued to grow and in just a few years was considered one of the highest-valued companies in the fashion world. As Tomas's business grew, Walk-On Shoes shrunk. They had stayed with the same styles year after year, ignoring the change in customer demand. It was not long before it became obvious that Tomas's business was keeping Walk-On afloat. During the production cycle, Tomas made it a practice to inspect the lines producing his shoes. During this inspection, he would engage in conversation with the supervisors. Two of the supervisors were his brothers-in-law. On one occasion, they cornered him, and in anger, Mikkel spouted out, "You owe everything to our dad."

"Ya," Nicolai chimed in. "Your money is coming at our father's expense."

Tomas looked them with disgust. He waved his hand and said, "You just don't get it, do you?" and walked away. The comments hurt, but Tomas felt it useless to engage in a debate he had already lost in their minds. However, their grumbling apparently found its way to Gustave's ears, for Tomas noticed a considerable cooling in his attitude toward him.

As Gustave's coolness turned to bitterness, Tomas wondered how he was to deal with this change in behavior. One night, Tomas had a vivid dream. It was similar to the dream he had years before on his way to Chicago. He awoke with a strong sensation that he should return to Wisconsin. So one day, he made a luncheon appointment with Rob, Henrika, and Elsa to talk things over with them. The three thought it unusual to be getting together during the day, and Rob, who was not shy about speaking his mind, said, "Are we about to engage in a clandestine mission?"

Tomas's face remained stoic as he began his explanation. Looking straight into Elsa and Henrika's eyes, he said, "Your father has turned against me. You know how hard I've worked for him, but he has been completely unscrupulous and has broken his wage contract with me again and again. But God has not permitted him to do me any harm! When I made changes to increase his business, he rewarded me by reducing my wages, but God has prospered me at your father's expense because of his stubborn refusal to change. When I left home for Chicago, I stayed overnight in Dodgeville. It was there that I made a decision to follow Jesus. I sensed then and I sense now that I should return home. I believe that the Lord is going to heal the rift between my brother and me. I don't know how, I just sense it."

Rob sat back in his chair and said, "Whew!"

Elsa and Henrika sat stunned for several moments, pondering the impact such a move would have on them. Finally, Elsa said, "I promised to be by your side whatever the circumstance."

Henrika spoke up and said, "I know my father has not treated you fairly, and now my brothers are poisoning his thinking. I believe it would be best to leave this place before their bitterness overtakes us."

Henrika and Elsa looked at each other and said in unison, "It's fine with us."

Elsa added, "So go ahead and do whatever God leads you to do."

*   *   *

Tomas fulfilled the years of obligation to Gustave and continued to build his company, Zurbriggen Classic Wear. Just as his father had done, Tomas was also building the work ethic into his boys. He gave them regular duties and had them report to one of the supervisors. Dan was fourteen now, and Nathan was twelve. Joseph, at six, was too young to work in the distribution center, but Elsa found many chores for him at home.

Tomas had a growing yearning to return to his childhood home, and since his obligation to Gustave was fulfilled, his desire burned even greater. He called Rob in his office one day to discuss a plan he was contemplating.

"Rob, our inventory is low right now, isn't it?"

"Yes, it always is at this time of the year. Why?"

"How long do you think it would take to load our inventory and equipment on semis?"

"Now what on earth is going on in that head of yours?"

"I want to move our operation."

"Where?"

"Back home to Chippewa Falls."

"Wow! That would take some pretty healthy planning. We would need a facility and a whole new staff. I'm sure all our people will not want to move. We would have to coordinate with all our suppliers and customers. It would be a big job."

"I know, that's why I have you."

"Gee, thanks for the vote of confidence."

"We haven't even discussed the hardest part."

"What's that?"

"When I left home, my brother was ready to kill me – literally! I need a smooth-talking ambassador to go to my brother and feel him out to see if my returning would cause problems."

Rob's eyes bulged out as he said, "And you want to throw me into the lion's den?"

"You are the man for the job. There's no fear, you're just the messenger. It's me who got run out of town. And while you're up there, if my brother isn't about to lynch me, I would want you to scout the area for a business location and find out if there is an available workforce."

"Are you sure that's all you want me to do? Just settle a twenty-year-old family feud and do the ground work for a company move."

"See," Tomas said, "when you say it like that, it doesn't sound too hard."

Rob went to Chippewa bearing presents for his father, mother, and his brother. Tomas, fearful of the outcome, spent much of his time in prayer and fasting. Late one night, he was in his den fervently praying for restoration with Marcus. As the night wore on, Tomas's eyes grew heavy, and he fell into a deep sleep. During that time, he dreamt that a man accosted him, and he argued and debated with him the entire night. Finally, the man said, "I must go, it's nearly dawn."

"No," Tomas replied, "not until you bless me!"

"What is your name?" he said.

"Tomas."

"How is it spelled?" the man asked.

"T-O-M-A-S," said Tomas as he spelled out the letters.

The man replied, "From this day forward, it will be spelled T-H-O-M-A-S. The H is to remind you of your encounter with the Holy One! And because you have been strong with God, you shall prevail among men." At that moment, Thomas fell from his couch, hit a footstool on his way to the floor, and knocked his hip out of joint. Elsa heard him scream in pain and came running. They transported him to the hospital, but for the rest of his life, he walked with a limp. Thomas was convinced that God gave him that injury as a reminder He would always be with him, and from that time on, he spelled his name with an H.

* * *

Rob spent a fair amount of time with the Zurbriggens. Becca wouldn't hear of him staying in a motel and insisted that he stay with them. After two weeks in Chippewa, he returned to Chicago and met with an anxious Thomas.

"Well, how did it go, Rob? How are my mom and dad? What happened when you talked with my brother?"

"Hold your horses, Thomas, one question at a time. Your parents are fine. Your dad is in good health, but his age is showing. Your mom is quite the hostess. I was treated like a visiting dignitary. They had a million questions. I filled them in on all you had done for your uncle and how he treated you. Your mother was so disgusted. She said, 'That ole skinflint!' They wanted to know all about your new company."

"What about Marcus?"

"Ah yes, Marcus." Rob stared at the ceiling just to heighten Thomas's excitement.

"Well!"

"Well, what?"

"Rob, if you don't stop yankin' my chain, I'm going to jump over this desk and take you to the floor."

Rob started laughing and replied, "Okay, here's the scoop. From the stories that you told me, I sense that Marcus has matured considerably. Of course he's now president of the company, and I understand it is doing well. He said he actually has missed not having a brother and would welcome the chance to build a relationship again."

Tears began to form in Thomas's eyes when he heard the news. "Oh, that's just great, Rob. I was afraid I would never see my family again. This is such good news."

"That's not all the good news I've got. I couldn't find a facility in Chippewa, but in the adjoining town of Eau Claire, an appliance manufacturer just vacated their facility. It has enough square footage to house our operation and allow for growth."

"What kind of price?"

"It's all here in this folder. I even got a lease. If you want it, sign the lease and send it back."

"Labor?"

"Ample supply of people looking for work. The wages up there are lower and the work ethic higher. A great combination."

"Rob, I think God wants me home. I'm going to drive up tomorrow."

*   *   *

The sun was just starting to set as Thomas approached the bridge over the Chippewa River. As he coasted down the bridge and onto Main Street, he slowed down to gaze at the Zurbriggen Leather Werks on his left. Nostalgia lifted his spirits as he remembered the years of his youth. Continuing up Main Street, he took in the familiar sights. A glance down a side street revealed Hoppe's Music Store, and there was the Boston Clothing Store on the corner. It brought back a memory of Ray Amdurski, the owner, and his commercials that always ended with "Large, Tall, or Small – We fit them all!" There was the dime store, then the next-door stairs leading to Dr. Brown's office, the eye doctor. Korgers was on the other side of the street. He remembered Grandpa Masses bringing boxes of little chickens out to the farm every spring. He always got them at Korgers. The Gamble Store was kitty-corner up the street across from Penny's, and the tin ice-cream cone was still in front of the dairy store. Farther up stood ole Chi-Hi, the high school. And at the corner, one of his favorite spots, the A&W root beer stand. He had been going there ever since all he could order was a baby root beer. He remembered that the owner sometimes substituted as the math teacher in junior high. Not able to resist the temptation, he pulled into the A&W and ordered a large root beer from the young lady who took his order right at his car.

After finishing his drink, he headed out on Highway 27 toward Cadott – toward home. As he turned onto the circle drive in front of his parents' house, he sat for a moment, soaking in the quiet country sounds. The soft chirping of crickets, the canopy of trees gently guarding the homestead, and the golden flow of light casting its beams from the windows out across the front porch. *What a difference from the Chicago atmosphere*, he thought.

Thomas got out of his car and slowly strolled down the walk. He stopped as he approached the house, feeling it odd to knock at the door of the home where he grew up. Footsteps sounded in the hallway, then the outside lights came on as the door opened, and he faced his mother for the first time in over two decades. When she recognized who was standing at her door, her hands flew up to her face in disbelief. Instead of hugging him or asking him to come in, she turned and ran down the hall, calling, "Papa, Papa, our boy, our boy has come home!"

Zachary stepped from his den and looked down the hallway, saying, "Oh my, oh my!"

Hugs and tears ensued as the three stood with their arms wrapped around each other, almost fearing that to let loose would cause separation again.

Finally, Zachary stood back and said, "Come in, son, and sit down. We want to hear everything about you."

"I thought Rob told you everything," Thomas replied.

"We want to hear it from you, Thomas," his mother said. "We want to hear your voice in our home again –"

Zachary interrupted, "You picked a good night to come, Thomas. Marcus will be here soon."

Thomas felt a lump form in his throat at the mention of Marcus, but he merely responded with, "Oh, he is."

A short time later, the front door opened, and loud footsteps came down the hall as Marcus called out, "Whose car is out in –" He stopped in midsentence as he entered the living room and saw Thomas. The two brothers stood staring at each other for three or four seconds; then Marcus ran across the room and threw his arms around Thomas. "Welcome home, brother," Marcus said.

An apprehensive Thomas responded with, "Thanks, Marcus. I appreciate that. Frankly, I didn't know what kind of reception I'd receive."

"We've all had much to learn, Thomas. The mistakes of our youth have cost us many years. Let's not let it cost us any more."

"I agree. I have a boatload of things I want to talk to you about."

"Let's meet for breakfast tomorrow," Marcus suggested. "Tonight we just need to be a family!"

*　　*　　*

A few days later, Thomas returned to Chicago, having leased an office, a distribution center, and an agreement for Zurbriggen Leather Werks to manufacture shoes for the "Z." Thomas initiated a flurry of activity in preparation for a move north. Shortly after his return, the last order of shoes was delivered from the Walk-On Shoe Company. Of course, Gustave was unaware that it was "literally" the last order. Elsa and Henrika were having difficulty dealing with emotions that were tugging at them from both directions. They knew their move must be kept secret, but keeping it from their mother was so painful, especially when they made what they knew would be their last visit for quite some time. It was during this visit that Elsa discovered a Pentacle[3] in her father's desk drawer. She knew her dad was a superstitious man, but she did not suspect he would put any substance into something like that. In a moment of haste, she stuck the Pentacle in her purse, determined to remove it from the house undetected.

In the following days, inventory was reduced as much as possible. Semitrucks were loaded with goods and equipment, and the caravan, led by Thomas, started for Wisconsin on Highway 14. Traffic was heavy on the first leg of the trip, making travel slow. It became very difficult to maintain contact with the semis and leave enough room for cars to pass them. Upon reaching Madison, they turned onto Highway 12 and, by evening, had reached the town of Baraboo where they found a motel and rested for the night.

*   *   *

Meanwhile, back in Chicago, Gustave became curious as to why he hadn't received additional orders from his son-in-law's order department. He stopped by Thomas's office only to discover it abandoned. He walked back to his car, puzzled and confused. As the reality of the situation sunk in, fear and anger welled up inside him. After questioning neighboring businesses, he learned moving trucks had left late that morning. They heard the company was moving north to Wisconsin. With anger and disgust, Gustave hurried to his house to inform his wife what had happened and that he was going to search for them. Before leaving the house, he went to his desk to retrieve his Pentacle. "Who was the last person in my office?" he demanded of his wife.

Nervously, she answered, "The girls were here yesterday, and Elsa made a phone call from there."

Gustave gritted his teeth and flew out the door. He stopped by the Walk-On factory, picked up several men, and set out in hot pursuit. It wasn't difficult to track a large caravan. Gustave surmised that they had taken Highway 14 north. When they reached a

---

[3]   Pentacle: From an *occult perspective*, it is representative of white magic and good. It also is supposed to represent man's intellect and reason.

truck stop on the Illinois-Wisconsin border, they talked with a Chicago-bound trucker who said he had passed a whole convoy of trucks heading north. Convinced they were on the right trail, they continued on.

It was about eight o'clock that evening. One of Gustave's men was driving, and Gustave, emotionally worn out from mental exhaustion, had fallen asleep. As he slept, a vivid dream encompassed him where he heard a warning from God to not harm Thomas. He felt God shaking him to get his attention but awoke to his driver tugging at his shoulder and pointing to a motel ahead surrounded by semis.

"That has to be them," Gustave shouted. "Pull in, pull in!"

Gustave quizzed the night clerk, telling him he was looking for his son-in-law. The part-time clerk was more interested in getting back to his TV program than preserving the security of his guests and quickly revealed Thomas's location. Gustave marched to the room and began pounding on the door. Thomas came to the door, surprised to see his father-in-law standing outside, surrounded by several large men.

An angry Gustave began shouting, "What do you mean by sneaking off like this, taking my daughters and rushing away? If you had to leave, why not have the courtesy to say farewell and let us have a going-away party? Why? I didn't even have a chance to kiss my grandchildren. This is sure a strange way to act! I'm so angry I'd like to beat you into the ground, and I would except . . ." Gustave caught his tongue before revealing his dream.

Gaining control of his anger, he lowered his emotional harangue a bit by saying, "I can understand your desire to return to the place where you grew up, but tell me, why did you sneak away like this, and why did you steal my Pentacle?"

By this time, Gustave was running out of steam, so Thomas took the opportunity to respond, "I sneaked away, Uncle Gus, because I was afraid of the scene you would make if I came and told you that we were moving. I thought you would try to turn Elsa against me just as you and your sons have turned on me. But as for your

Pentacle, I have no use for such a thing. If you can find it or any other possession of yours, I will give it back without question and punish the one who took it." Thomas did not know that Elsa had taken the Pentacle from Gustave's desk, so he said, "Feel free to search our rooms. We have nothing to hide."

Gustave took him up on it and searched Rob and Henricka's room first and then Thomas' room. As he searched, Elsa remained seated on the bed for she had hidden the Pentacle in her pillow. When Gustave came to where she was seated Elsa explained, "Forgive me for not getting up, Daddy, but I'm pregnant and not feeling well."

Gustave shook his head in acknowledgement and passed her by.

After they finished, Thomas, feeling humiliated by Gustave's accusation, said, "What did you find? You came rushing after me as if I'm some criminal. You have searched through everything. Now put everything I stole out here in front of us, before your men and mine, for all to see. Twenty years I've been with you, and all that time everything I did was to help you prosper. I worked in the factory. I worked nights, weekends, whatever it took to grow Walk-On. Yes, twenty years – fourteen building your business and six earning the Coolee *and* Pro-fessional labels. And you reduced my wages ten times. I know, except for the grace of God, you would have sent me off without a penny to my name. God has seen your cruelty, Gustave, and He has seen my hard work. I believe the Lord has used me to accomplish His plan, and I would hate to be the one who resisted God's plan."

Gustave replied, "These women are my daughters, and these children are my grandchildren. All you have, you have because of me. It's mine – all of it is mine!" Gustave lowered his arms in defeat and said, "But I have to admit, you have me at a disadvantage. What am I to do? Shall I harm my own daughters and grandchildren?" Then Gustave extended his hand and said, "No, let's have peace between us!"

Thomas grasped his hand, saying, "That sounds very good. Why don't you and your men join us for a dinner to celebrate our agreement?"

"That would be very nice," he replied.

As they gathered in the dining room, Thomas stood and said, "I do not claim any of these possessions. For some unknown reason, God chose to bless me. I am but a manger of what He has placed under my care. Please join me in a prayer of thanksgiving to our benevolent God."

The next morning, Gustave rose early, kissed his daughters and grandchildren, and returned home.

CHAPTER 11

Life

AFTER GUSTAVE DEPARTED, Thomas and the caravan continued north, passing a Heileman Brewery sign depicting the slogan, "This is God's Country." Thomas remarked, "It sure is, but not because of Heileman." Late that afternoon, they reached the city of Eau Claire, Wisconsin. Immediately, they began to search for temporary lodging for themselves and the crew. In a few days, everyone was settled, then for the next month, Rob and Thomas worked tirelessly, setting up the new facility.

The task of seeking permanent housing fell to Elsa and Henrika. The couples had decided to rent until they became acquainted with the community and had time to look for a home with their husbands. Each day, the ladies called ads in the paper and made appointments to see houses. They were thrilled when they found two homes for rent only three blocks apart.

Elsa rented a three-bedroom bungalow. It was light green stucco with white trim on the fascia and on the doors and windows. It had nice shrubbery around the house and a two-car garage in the back. The inside needed what Thomas called "Lipstick and Rouge," for the house showed the results of being a rental.

Henrika found a pretty white colonial trimmed with black shutters. The house was set off in front with a white picket fence. She was fortunate to find a family that was going to be gone for six months, and as an owner-occupied home, it was much cleaner and in better condition than Elsa's.

As Henrika and the children were moving in and setting up the house, a teenage girl stopped by to meet the new neighbors. "Hi, I'm Kelley. I live just across the street."

"Hello, Kelley," Henrika said. "I'm Mrs. Buchanan, and these are two of my sons, Rueben and Simon, and my daughter, Dinah."

"Well, ah, welcome to the neighborhood. It will be nice to have a girl my age across the street."

"It nice to meet you too," Dinah politely answered.

"Ah, Dinah, there's a good movie on TV tomorrow night. I've seen it before but would like to see it again. It's called *Please Don't Eat the Daisies* with Doris Day. If your mother says it's okay, would you like to come over and watch it with me?"

Dinah looked over at her mother for an indication of permission, and Henrika said, "As long as it's just across the street. It's good to make friends with the neighbors."

The next evening, after Dinah finished setting up her bedroom, she said to her mom, "I'm going across the street now to watch that movie with Kelley."

"Okay, dear, come home right after it's over."

"I will," she answered and skipped out the door and across the street.

Kelley met her at the door and invited her in. "How about making some popcorn for the movie?" Kelley asked.

Dinah said, "That sounds good."

As they were heating the pan, a young man came into the room. Kelley said, "Dinah, this is my older brother, Carl. He's home from college for the summer."

"Hey, Dinah, good to have a pretty-lookin' girl move into the neighborhood."

Dinah didn't know if she should be flattered or not because his familiar manner made her feel uncomfortable.

When the popcorn was done, Kelley looked in the refrigerator and noticed they were out of soda. "Dinah," she said, "I'm going to run down to the neighborhood store and get some pop. The movie will be starting soon. Why don't you tune it in so you don't miss the beginning? I'll be back in fifteen."

Dinah carried the bowl of popcorn to the living room, turned on the TV, and settled down at the end of the sofa. Carl sauntered into the room and sprawled out on the couch, uncomfortably close to Dinah.

"So where do you come from, Dinah?" Carl asked.

Dinah tried to slide over while nervously replying, "Chicago."

"Bet you had a lot of boyfriends down there, huh?"

"No," she answered, becoming even more uncomfortable.

"Oh, come on, a big city girl with no boyfriends. I don't believe it."

As he said that, he slid a little closer and slipped his arm around Dinah's shoulders.

*   *   *

Henrika was making supper a little later than usual because of the long hours Rob was putting in. It was after seven o'clock when he pulled into the drive. Tired from another day of laborious work, he slowly slid one foot out of the car and then the other, taking a moment to enjoy the end of a hard day when he heard Dinah screaming as she came running across the street, crying hysterically.

"Honey, what's the matter?" he asked as she flew into his arms.

She tried to talk, but her incessant sobbing prevented her from speaking coherently. Rob noticed that her dress was torn, and her hair was disheveled, so he said again, "What is it, Dinah? What happened to you?"

Dinah was trying hard to gain some control and managed to say, "K-Kelley's b-brother."

By this time, Henrika heard the commotion and came out to see what was going on. Seeing her daughter so distraught, she ran to her and asked, "Dinah, what's wrong, sweetheart?"

Dinah inhaled deeply trying to stop sobbing and said, "Kelley's brother . . . he raped me!"

Rob said, "He what?"

"Kelley went to the neighborhood store to get some soda," Dinah explained. "She said it would only take a few minutes. We were going to watch a movie. I stayed at the house so I wouldn't miss the first part. After she left, her brother came in the room and sat real close to me. He started talking weird, asking me about boyfriends, and suddenly . . ."

Dinah shook as she inhaled a shaky sobbing breath before beginning again.

"Suddenly he pushed me down on the couch and pulled my panties off."

That's all Rob had to hear, "Henrika, call the police," he shouted as he ran across the street. As he reached the neighbor's front door, Kelley was returning from the store. He noticed she was carrying a six-pack of soda. Making the connection, he said, "Are you Kelley?"

Kelley, unaware of what was happening nervously said, "Yes, why?"

"Is your brother in the house?"

"Yes, I think so."

"Take me to him!"

"Who are you?" Kelley asked, for she had not met Rob and was growing more confused with each question.

"Dinah's father," he said loudly. "Take me to your brother!"

Kelley hesitated, but Rob shouted, "*Now!*" His authoritative insistence stirred Kelley to action. She quickly opened the door, and Rob dashed in the house. His unexpected presence startled Carl, who was just coming from the bathroom.

"Are you Kelley's brother?" Rob demanded.

"Ya," he replied, "Who are you?"

"What did you do to my little girl, you pervert?"

Realizing this man was the father of the girl he assaulted, he bolted out the door with Rob at his heels. Halfway across the front lawn, Rob lunged and pinned him to the ground. As the two were scuffling, a squad car pulled up. The policemen ran over and pulled them apart, handcuffed both of them, and leaned them over the squad car, one on the front, and the other on the back.

"That pervert raped my daughter," Rob shouted. "We're the ones who called you!"

It took an hour of questioning by the police to get everyone's statements and sort things out. Dinah was taken to the hospital, and Kelley's brother was arrested.

Physically, Dinah recovered, but it left emotional scars that stayed with her for a lifetime. Rob and Henrika decided that living there provided an ever constant reminder of the tragedy and that it would be better to move away, so they packed up their belongings and moved again.

*   *   *

The incident with Dinah brought the Buchanans and the Zurbriggens even closer together than before, and it brought them closer to God. The families eventually found a place to worship after attending several churches in the area. It was on the outskirts of Chippewa Falls. The chapel, as it was called, was led by Pastor Bill Pederson, a quiet, sensitive, pious man with a remarkable ability to bring deep meaning out of the scriptures. His wife and helpmate, Ruby, complimented their ministry by displaying a sincere love for people.

One Sunday morning, the church had arranged for a special speaker. Adam Overgard, a missionary to the country of Zaire, presented the trials and victories of bringing Christ to a nation in political unrest. The Zurbriggens asked Adam to come to their home following the service. After dinner, they were visiting outside on the patio when Adam said, "Thomas, I have a strong impression that I believe is from God."

"Somewhat surprised yet curious, Thomas asked, "What do you mean?"

"This happens occasionally in Zaire. I may be preaching, and I receive a forceful inclination to preach something other than what I have prepared, or I may be calling on a family and sense that there is involvement in witchcraft. Then there are times when I'm visiting with someone, and I feel God is going to use that person in our work. As we have been visiting, I have a sense the Lord is going to use you in a tremendous way. I'm not sure, but I feel it is because you have honored God in the past." I believe that God is going to do something through you because you give Him the glory. I also have the sense that a strong, Godly man will come from your family."

Thomas, being somewhat skeptical, replied, "What makes you think this is from God?"

Adam replied, "Like I said, I have an inclination. My advice is never to take man's word unless you verify. Check what I have said with the scriptures, pray for wisdom to understand, and ask someone who is of high spiritual character for guidance. If there is no conflict, it is probably true."

*   *   *

It was two in the morning. Elsa awoke in pain, "Thomas!" she screamed.

A drowsy Thomas lifted his head and said, "Huh? What's the matter?"

"Thomas, it's time, my water broke, and I'm bleeding!"

Thomas bolted from the bed, trying to clear his head.

"Call my sister and tell her to come to the house," Elsa directed, "hurry."

Thomas quickly made the call, grabbed Elsa's suitcase, and helped her to the car. The hospital was not far, but Elsa moaned at every little bump in the road. When they arrived at the emergency entrance, the doctor on duty took one look and rushed her upstairs.

Rob dropped Henrika off at her sister's house and came directly to the hospital to be with Thomas in the waiting room. Hours never went by so slowly as they did that morning and afternoon.

Thomas nervously paced the floor of the waiting room.

"All your pacing isn't going to speed up the process," Rob advised. "Why don't you have a cup of coffee?"

"I'm up to my gills in coffee," Thomas shot back. "What on earth could be taking so long? I'm going out to the nurses' station."

Thomas stopped the nurse he thought was in charge and asked, "Have you any news about my wife? This is unusual isn't it, I mean the length of time?"

"I'll see if the doctor will give me a report, sir," she replied. "Have a seat in the waiting room, and I'll be right back."

In a few minutes, the nurse returned. "Mr. Zurbriggen, the doctor said that Elsa is going through a very difficult delivery, but he expected it would be no more than an hour before the baby will be born."

The afternoon crept into evening, evening into the night, and night into the morning. It was twenty-two hours from the time they entered the hospital when the doctor finally appeared in the waiting room.

"Mr. Zurbriggen," he began, "Can we slip into the counseling room? It's more private in there."

As they left the waiting room, Rob followed. Thomas, noticing the doctor's puzzled expression, said, "It's okay, he's my best friend."

"Doc, what's going on?" Thomas asked.

"Well," the doctor said, hesitating a moment to search for words, "You're the father of a healthy baby boy."

Thomas's face lit up with pride. He slapped Rob and said, "It's another boy!"

Then the doctor said, "I am so sorry, sir," sadness covered the doctor's face as he continued, "We did all that we could for your wife."

Thomas's face changed from a bright beaming smile to one grave concern.

"Mr. Zurbriggen," the doctor continued, "as you know, the delivery was very long. A birth like that is very taxing."

"Well, how is she? How is Elsa?"

"Sir, I'm sorry, your wife didn't make it through the delivery."

Thomas felt like someone punched him in the chest as he fell back against the couch, numbed with disbelief. "No," he muttered, "not my Elsa. What . . . what happened?"

The doctor went into a long explanation, but Thomas didn't hear any of it.

Rob grabbed hold of him and held him as his body shook from sobbing. Rob held him for a long time, saying nothing, just holding him. They left the hospital with Rob's arm still around his friend's shoulder and went back to Thomas's house with the unpleasant task of telling his children that their mom wasn't coming home.

Gustave Soderstom, his wife, and sons drove up from Chicago to be with and grieve with the rest of the family. Pastor Bill conducted the funeral and used his love for God and his love for people to tell those gathered how they could spend eternity in heaven.

"Friends," Pastor Bill began, "there are many reasons for a funeral. It provides a time for family and friends to mourn and to show respect for the departed one. But there is another reason that all too often is overlooked. King Solomon said there is a time for everything, a time to live and a time to die. Today, my friends, is also a time to look at yourselves. A time to ask yourself, 'If I were to die tonight, where would I go? Where would I spend eternity?' It's a legitimate question and one that should be answered. Some of you may say, 'Why, I've gone to church all my life and been baptized. I'm okay!' Others would reason, 'I'm not such a bad person. I think the good I've done will outweigh the bad!' I'm here to tell you that going to church, baptized or not, will no more help you make it to heaven than going in a garage will make you a car! Furthermore, there's no one who can show me in the Bible where God weighs your good deeds against your sin as a pass into heaven because it just isn't there! That's a boldface lie from the pit of hell!

"So one of the reasons for a funeral is so you may receive God's invitation, to hear His plan for your eternal life. Listen to the truth of what God says about us, yes, all of us. In Romans 3:23, God says, 'For all have sinned and fall short of the glory of God.' Did you hear that crucial word in there? He said *all* have sinned. That means me, and it means you!

"Also, in Romans the sixth chapter and the twenty-third verse, it says, 'For the wages of sin is death' – meaning hell – 'but the gift of God is eternal life in Christ Jesus our Lord.' Friends and family, today that gift can be yours. When the time comes to lay your body in a casket, you can be assured that your soul will have already been taken to heaven to be with our Lord Jesus.

"You see, John 3:3 says, 'No one can see the kingdom of God unless he is born again.' "Born again," what does that mean? It means to have a spiritual encounter with Jesus. It means accepting the fact that Jesus died on a cross to pay for each and every wrong thing that you have ever done or will do.

"I haven't known the Zurbriggens very long, but I know this. Elsa is present with the Lord Jesus as we speak, and I know that Thomas, when he dies, will be in the same place. You might ask, how can I know this? I know it by the testimony of their mouths. They both confessed Jesus as their Savior, and the Bible says that is being born again. So I ask you, would you like to know where you will spend eternity? I would love to spend time with you to sort it out. Please talk to me after the service if you want to know more. Now let's pray together."

The week after Elsa's funeral, Henrika, Rob, and Thomas went to the hospital to bring his new son home. Thomas named him Benjamin.

*   *   *

Getting back to normal after a tragedy or a loss is easier to say than to do, as Thomas was finding out. He had to find a nurse-babysitter to care for his children and to run his household. He had put his own emotions on hold due to the family's needs, but now, even with the demand of the business, he spent many nights in agony over the loss of his beloved Elsa. But God provides ways to overcome heartache. He promises that we will not have to endure more than we can bear and will provide stepping-stones to lead us out of sorrow and trouble.[4]

During this time, Thomas and Rob had become closer than brothers. Their talents complimented each other perfectly. They worked together and played together. When one hurt, the other hurt. They truly grew to love one another. Rob became a stepping stone for Thomas.

---

[4]   I Corinthians 10:13

CHAPTER 12

Life – It Isn't Always a Picnic!

PART OF THE difficulty of moving their headquarters was establishing a financial relationship with a local bank. Zurbriggen Classic Wear needed a financial institution large enough to handle a growing company, yet with enough local authority to be able to make decisions without having to wait three to four weeks while requests were decided in some far-off corporate wilderness. They decided on the Marshall & Isley Bank, better known as M & I Bank. Conrad Pritchard, the bank president, was a tall, broad-shouldered man. His graying hair and neatly trimmed mustache gave him a distinction that added to his natural command of authority. Thomas and Rob developed a personal relationship with Conrad, and when the company had their summer picnic at Irvin Park in Chippewa, Conrad and his wife were invited.

The picnic included blow-up inflatables and games for the children and adults alike. Softball, a beanbag toss, an abundance of food and soda provided something for everyone. After they had played and eaten and laughed and grown tired, an awards ceremony was held. There were awards for the most improved, the most helpful, and half dozen other categories.

During the day, Conrad had participated in many of the games and left Mrs. Pritchard, Evelyn, to find her own amusement. Evelyn was a strikingly beautiful woman. She had been runner up to Miss Wisconsin thirty years before and still maintained an appearance that turned men's heads. As her husband joined in the picnic games, Evelyn found her own pastime. She struck up a conversation with Ruben, Rob's oldest son, earlier in the day. The two seemed to be thoroughly enjoying one another's company. So much so that during the awards ceremony, they stole off to a remote section of the park and in the shelter of the underbrush became intimate. As the awards ceremony was concluding, they rejoined the gathering feeling perfectly secure that no one was the wiser.

The next Monday, one of the company's accountants came to Thomas's office and asked to speak with him. Thomas's secretary checked with her boss and then told him to go right in. He nervously pulled at his necktie as Thomas asked, "Leonard, what is it that you wanted to discuss with me?"

"Well, sir," he choked out, "I hardly know where to begin. Would you mind, sir, if we closed the door?"

Thomas, recognizing he must have something of consequence on his mind, stood and made his way to his office door and said, "Leonard, why don't you start at the beginning?"

"Sir, we really appreciate you throwing a picnic for us. It was great fun."

"Thank you, Leonard. It's really me who is thankful for the great job you and the other employees do around here."

"Mr. Zurbriggen, what I have to say is very difficult, but I feel that I, I . . ." He looked down at the floor unable to continue his sentence.

"Leonard, please relax. Whatever it is, I'll listen. Please go on."

"Well, I ate a bit too much at the picnic, and so during the awards ceremony, I took a walk to help digest the food. I was walking by the forested end of the park when I heard some moaning coming from the underbrush. I thought someone might have needed help, so I quietly made my way to where the sound was coming from, and that's when I saw them." Leonard stopped his explanation abruptly until Thomas urged him to continue.

"Sir, it was Mr. Buchanan's son."

"Rob's son?"

"Yes, sir. His son, Rueben."

"What was he doing?"

"He was, you know, he was with Mrs. Pritchard on the ground."

Thomas was nearly speechless, but he pressed for more information. "Leonard, could you tell if Mrs. Pritchard was there by her own choice?"

"At the time, I didn't know, sir, because I hightailed it out of there, but later, I saw them walk back to the ceremony together, acting very friendly. I hope I haven't overstepped my boundaries, Mr. Zurbriggen. It was just bothering me, so I felt I had to tell someone, and I didn't know how to approach Mr. Buchanan."

"Not at all, Leonard. I appreciate how difficult this must have been for you, and I thank you for doing the right thing."

Leonard nodded and said, "Thank you for listening," and he turned and left the office.

Thomas sat back in his chair, realizing how difficult it must have been for Leonard, because he knew how difficult it was going to be for him. He walked slowly over to Rob's office and knocked on the door.

"Hey, buddy," Rob said in his friendly way. "Come on in."

"Rob, I have to tell you something very unpleasant, and we have to figure out how we are going to handle it."

Thomas's serious tone immediately got Rob's attention, and he motioned for him to sit down.

Thomas related the incident as Leonard had told it and said, "Rob, we have two people we have to deal with, Reuben and Conrad."

Rob put his elbows on his desk and laid his head in his hands. "My heart . . . it's . . . it's broken, Thomas. What on earth are we going to do?"

After a long silence, Thomas said, "First, I think we should call Reuben in and confront him. If he admits to this, I believe we have to call Conrad and ask him if he and his wife could meet with us at our office. I think we should have Rueben at that meeting as well."

"Oh, that could be messy," Rob sighed.

"Sometimes the truth gets that way, Rob. I think Conrad deserves to know the truth, and both Reuben and Evelyn should face the consequences."

* * *

They went ahead with the plan, and as expected, it was messy. Conrad arrived with Evelyn, puzzled over the unusual request to bring his wife. As they were shown into Thomas's office, Thomas rose from his desk, welcomed them, and asked them to be seated. Before Conrad could question the reason for the meeting, Rob entered, followed by his son. At the sight of Rueben, Evelyn nervously fidgeted in her seat.

"Conrad, Mrs. Pritchard," Thomas began, I apologize for the mysterious manner in which I called this meeting, but as you will learn, it is of a very sensitive and private nature."

"You certainly know how to create suspense, Thomas," Conrad stated.

"Conrad," Rob began, "it has come to our attention from an eyewitness that . . ." and Rob continued to relate the episode between Evelyn and Rueben.

"This can't be! Is there any truth to this, Evelyn?" She buried her head in her hands and didn't respond. Feeling betrayed, Conrad lashed out at Rueben, "Why you, filthy gigolo, I ought to thrash the life out of you," he said, jumping up from his chair with his fist clenched.

"Hold on a moment, Conrad!" Thomas yelled as he and Rob jumped up and stood in front of Rueben.

"Go ahead, coddle your own. You're despicable. I sure misjudged the two of you."

"We are dealing with Rueben. He is not getting through this without paying a price, Conrad. As your friend, we felt it must be brought to your attention. And since it was mutual, we had no other choice."

"Well, was it?" Conrad shouted at Evelyn. "Tell me, did he force himself on you?"

Evelyn started to cry but gave no answer.

Conrad grabbed her by the arm and exited the office, nearly faster than Evelyn's feet could move.

Conrad was shocked and angry, first at Rueben, then at Rob and Thomas, and then with his wife. He was a proud man, and this humiliated him. Eventually, it cost his marriage, especially after he found out that her dalliances were occurring on a regular basis. It nearly forced Thomas and Rob to secure other banking services, but a few months after his divorce, Conrad called and asked to meet with them. At the meeting, he apologized for the things he had said and asked for their forgiveness.

Reuben was counseled by his dad and his Uncle Thomas to repent of his wrongdoing. Then he was given a choice. He could receive a demotion at work and do one hundred hours of community service, or be fired. He reluctantly chose the demotion.

* * *

The phone call came on a hot August afternoon. There was a quiet sobbing on the other end. Thomas answered and said, "Hello, who is this?" There was no answer. "Hello," he said again, "is something wrong?"

"Thomas," came a weak reply, "this is Mom. Papa has died."

"Oh, Mom, I'll be right there!"

On the way, Thomas prayed, "Oh Lord, I can't handle any more tragedies. Lord, what am I to do? I am so weak, and this is too much for me to bear." Tears filled his eyes, forcing him to pull over to the side of the road. He sat there with his head against the steering wheel, softly crying, when a knock sounded on the window. It was a local policeman.

"Sir, are you all right?" he asked.

Thomas reached for his handkerchief, blew his nose, and said, "No! My father just died. I'm on my way to be with my mother, but I just had to stop."

"I'm sorry to hear that. What was his name?"

"Zurbriggen, Zachary Zurbriggen."

The policeman stepped back, visibly stunned. "I knew your father. He was a great man in my book. When I was in the police academy, my wife had a baby. We had no way to pay the hospital expenses, so I was going to drop out of the academy to take a job. Somehow, I never knew how, your father learned of my predicament and paid the hospital bill for us. I tried to repay him, but he wouldn't take a cent. Ya know what he said to me?"

"No, I don't."

"He said, 'Young man, you just be the best policeman you can be, that is payment enough.' Can I ask your name?"

"It's Thomas."

"Well, Thomas, I am very sorry to learn of Mr. Zurbriggen's death. Is there anything that I can do? Could I drive you somewhere?"

Thomas looked up at the policeman and said, "You've already done it, officer. Your story encouraged me. It gave me another good memory of my dad. To be truthful, I had just told God that I have had it. My wife died a short time ago, now my dad. It all washed over me like a tidal wave, but I believe God sent a policeman to lift my spirits. I don't know how to explain it, but this has lifted my spirits."

"That's good, and, Thomas, telling you that story made my day. Thank you!"

"No," Thomas said, "thank God for bringing us together."

"I will do that. Please tell your mom that Peter Bradward sends his sympathy."

"I'll do that, Peter. Good day."

Thomas continued on to his parents' home and did all he could for his mother. Later that night, he sat on the porch with his mom. He was thinking that this move north proved to be full of heartaches. The attack on Dinah, the incident with Reuben, and God taking Elsa and his father home – all produced a deep sadness.

Thomas held his mother in his arms as they gently swung on the old porch swing. In trying to provide some comfort, he said to her, "Mom, life is hard!" His mother looked up at him and replied, "Son, if it were easy, we wouldn't need God."

CHAPTER 13

Love of a Father

"IT HAS BEEN said, 'time heals all wounds.' I do not agree. The wounds remain. In time, the mind, protecting its sanity, covers them with scar tissue and the pain lessens. But it is never gone."[5]

Protecting his sanity certainly described the emotional condition of Thomas Zurbriggen. Living through the past events forced him to focus on the blessings in his life or be sucked into the miry pit. After all, he had his children and a new baby boy to consider, and being back in familiar territory among family brought a sense of peace and comfort.

Joseph was now seventeen, and just as his adopted brothers, his cousins, and his Uncle Marcus and his father before him, Joseph was put to work doing menial cleanup jobs around the business. Each day, he had prescribed tasks to complete in different areas of the facility. It provided ample opportunity to observe what was

---

[5] Rose F. Kennedy

happening out in the warehouse and away from the office. He soon learned the his older brothers and cousins were taking advantage of the family name and skipping out of work early. They had devised ways to prevent detection by covering for each other. When Joseph became aware of their scheme, he reported it to his dad.

It was common knowledge that Thomas favored Joseph. It wasn't right, but it was true. One could rationalize the favoritism was the result of attempting to have children naturally and the pent-up anxiety the failure produced, contrasted with being blessed by a natural child after giving up hope. It didn't justify favoritism, but it did explain it. Thomas was grateful to learn of the deception being orchestrated by the other boys and disciplined them appropriately. And for Joseph, he was rewarded by becoming the "Z" poster boy in the company's new national ad campaign, which by the way, gave Joseph considerable notoriety. The other boys, having been taken to the proverbial woodshed, were, needless to say, extremely resentful. They hated Joseph because of their father's partiality and verbally harassed him constantly.

This harsh treatment bothered Joseph to the point of giving him nightmares. One day, when the heckling grew intense, Joseph lashed back. "There will come a day when you'll come begging on your knees to me!" he shouted.

"Oh ya, and when might that day be?" Simon asked in jest.

"I had a dream that I will be in charge some day," Joseph lashed back. "We'll see what kind of tune you'll be singing then."

"So you want to be our boss, do you? You cocky little wimp!" Nathan spewed out. "That'll be the day when hell freezes over."

Joseph didn't seem to connect the fact that when he made these outlandish claims the boys chided him all the more, in fact, some time later, he bragged to them about another dream. "You imbeciles will be groveling in front of me when my day comes," he warned.

"What day will that be?" they chortled. "Is it when the men in white suits come to take you away?"

"No," Joseph shouted, trying to bolster a defense. "It's when a crowd of people and my whole family will stand and applaud my actions."

"We're tired of hearing this drivel," they said and turned their backs in disgust. Sometime later, when Joseph was with his dad, he told Thomas about the dreams. Thomas rebuked him, saying, "Joseph, don't you know pride goes before the fall?" His brothers and cousins were fit to be tied over this pompous little fool, but deep down, Thomas secretly wondered if there was some meaning to these dreams.

*   *   *

All who love fashion dream of attending the greatest fashion shows. There are four locations that are regarded as the best. The most talked about and highly revered fashion shows are held each year in London, Paris, Milan, and New York. This gives a good overall view of the fashion of the world. It could be said the world's fashion is influenced by these four locations. Zurbriggen Classic Wear was appearing in the New York show this year, and they were unveiling an entirely new line, hoping to upstage foreign and eastern designers. Thomas had sent his sons and their cousins ahead to make arrangements and set up for the show. He was going to attend himself, but not until opening day. Anxious to hear how the setup was going, he called Joseph to his office and arranged for him to fly to New York and send a report back to him.

Joseph arrived in New York the next day and made his way to the Lincoln Center. Promotion of Fashion Week was in full swing. Names renown in the fashion world were flashing across the lighted marquee in front of the center. Joseph paused to observe the competition his father would be facing. The sign lit up with the face of Oscar de la Renta and a tag line, "Famous for casual luxury." Next was Mary Quant, creator of the miniskirt. Then Pierre Cardin, creator of futuristic fashions, space-age catsuits, body stockings, Beatle suits, and cutout dresses. The promo following Pierre caught Joseph by surprise when his own face splashed across the marquee captioned by "Classic Wear by Zurbriggen, creator of the "Z," a total fashion experience! He beamed with pride as he imagined his brothers and cousins seeing his face projected for all New York to see.

When he entered the building, he was stopped a security guard. As he showed his identification, he pointed up to the sign displaying his face. The guard nodded his head and said, "I thought you looked familiar."

Joseph asked, "Could you direct me to the Zurbriggen area?"

"I can," the guard said, "but you'll not find anyone there."

"Why not?" Joseph asked, puzzled by the response.

"Oh, those boys are making the most of their time in New York. I heard them say they were headed for Studio 54."

"What is that?" Joseph asked.

"It's one of the trendy nightclubs," the guard replied. "Come outside. I'll hail you a cab. They'll take you right to the place."

Joseph thanked the security guard and climbed into the cab. Fifteen minutes later, they pulled in front of Studio 54. As Joseph got out of the car, two of his brothers and several cousins stumbled through the front door, howling like a bunch of banshees. When Dan spotted Joseph, he let out a squeal and said, "Lookee here who's come to spoil our fun."

The others gathered around, yelling insults and threats, the result of too much liquor. One of them yelled out with slurred speech, "Hey, let's take weeny boy's cab to the hotel," and with that, suggestion they all piled into the cab. The cab driver was yelling something in another language, but no one paid attention to him. Finally, Joseph told the driver to haul them to the hotel where they were registered, and off they went.

Joseph paid the driver as his boisterous family piled out of the cab and nosily tramped through the lobby to the elevator. They had rented a luxurious suite on the top floor of the hotel. The suite included a miniature swimming pool, hot tubs, and bathrooms in each bedroom. The kitchen and bar were fully stocked, and the décor could only be described as opulent.

Evidence of riotous living was strewn throughout the suite. Liquor bottles, half-eaten food, clothes, and other debris littered the interior. Joseph had just closed the door when Simon yelled out, "How 'bout we get some girls?"

A chorus of "Ya, man, good idea," chimed in agreement.

Joseph, appalled by the lascivious behavior of his brothers and cousins, protested to them, saying, "You know Dad would never approve of this behavior. He sent me to report on the setup, but when I asked where to find you, even the security guard at the center said you were out partying. You're going to be in deep trouble when Dad hears about this!

The thought of having to explain their behavior to Thomas had a sobering effect of the group. Nathan spoke up and tried to reason with Joseph. "Little Joe," he began, "I admit we did get carried away a bit, but it's our first time in the Big Apple, and I guess like most small town kids, we went overboard."

"Ya," Dan echoed, "we went overboard. Come back to the center with us. Were all set up. You'll see that we have been working hard."

Joseph agreed, and they proceeded back to the Lincoln Center, but on the way, the brothers and cousins concocted a plan to rid themselves of this little troublemaker once and for all.

Jude said, "Let's take him out in the back alley and do away with the dreamer. It's New York, we can tell our fathers that he got mugged."

Rueben objected to such a brutal attack on one within the family. He suggested they tie him up, gag him, and throw him the supply closet assigned to their company. "In a day or so, he'll be too afraid to give a bad report."

They all agreed to the devious plot and preceded to take Joseph to the area in the center the models used to change garments. As they approached the supply closet, Dan stepped in first and motioned for Joseph to follow. Jude pinned Joseph's arms from behind as he stepped into the room, and Simon stretched duct tape across his mouth. They stripped off his designer "Z" attire down to his underwear while Nathan wrapped a rope around his legs and tied his hands behind his back.

As they pushed him to the floor, Dan sneered, "Maybe this will give you time to think about that report you're supposed to make," and they locked the door behind them.

*   *   *

Participants in the style show were from several countries around the world. One of the exhibitors was a firm from Colombia, South America. It was also the first time they had entered the show and had brought with them a number of workers who were at best indiscriminate but acted as outright hoodlums. Much of their time was spent lingering about in areas where they had no business. Unknown to the show's promoters, the Colombian company was using the show as a front to smuggle cocaine into the United States. In their attempt to hide the illicit drugs, they looked for areas away from their company's assigned space, in the event of discovery, it could not be traced back to them. Noticing no one around the Zurbriggen area, they picked the lock to the "Z's" supply room, and to their surprise, found a young man gagged and bound, lying on the floor.

"What is this?" one of the Colombians exclaimed.

"A gift!" another added.

They hurriedly dumped their stash in an empty cabinet in the back of the room and placed a lock on it, figuring that no one would question a locked cabinet. Their leader motioned for his companions to quietly pick Joseph up while he checked to see if the hallway was clear. Joseph would soon discover that cocaine wasn't their only enterprise.

*   *   *

Rueben did not go to the center with the others. He didn't have the stomach for such things, but the next morning, he got up early and went to the center alone with the intention of freeing his brother. He unlocked the door, expecting to find Joseph inside, but he had vanished. Reuben frantically searched the room, his heart pounding with fear. *Where is he? Where could he be?* he wondered, confused by the disappearance. In desperation, he rushed back to the hotel and burst into the suite, hollering, "Wake up, wake up. Joseph is gone!"

Several sleepy heads rose off their pillows, wondering what all the yelling was about. Simon mumbled, "What? What's all the hollering?"

"Get up, all of you!" Reuben pleaded. "Joseph has disappeared."

Dan and Nathan staggered from their bedroom, saying, "Gone? Did you say Joseph's gone?"

Rueben fell to his knees, crying, "What are we going to do? Dad is going to kill us."

Jude, the one who wanted to take Joseph to the alley, said, "Let's call the cops and report him missing. Then we'll call home and tell the story of him getting here, but being anxious to go back to the center and left before we were up. We can truthfully tell them that Rueben went to the center to check on him, but he wasn't there."

"Good idea," said Dan. "That's the story we'll stick with. Hey, this is our answer. We've wanted to get rid of the little snitch for a long time. Now someone has done it for us, and our hands are clean!"

Nathan called the police, but they wouldn't investigate until a person had been missing for twenty-four hours. Nathan said to Reuben, "It was your idea to tie him up in the closet, so it's your job to call Dad."

A guilt-ridden Reuben dialed the number. When Thomas answered, Reuben broke down and sobbed, "It's Joseph, he's missing. We can't find him anywhere."

Thomas felt his heart tearing at the inside of his chest as he screamed, "No, no . . . not my Joseph! He's probably lost. Call the police. Please tell me he's just lost. Reuben . . . he's just lost. You must find him!"

The police did come and investigate but found no trace of Joseph. Several witnesses remembered seeing him the day before, but no one saw him the morning he vanished. Thomas and Rob arrived in New York and immediately met with the police. Rob took over managing the show, while Thomas insisted the police interview each of the boys separately in an effort to find some clue to aid in the investigation.

Thomas stayed in New York for three weeks after the show was over, determined to find his boy, but no leads were forthcoming.

A broken-hearted, dejected father left the city with a weight of sorrow pushing him down again into the pit. His family tried to comfort him, but it was no use. "I will die mourning for my son," he would say. For weeks, he did not go to work. During that time, he didn't shave or have contact with anyone outside his home. When encouraged to come back to work, all he would say is, "Life has delivered more than I can bear!"

CHAPTER 14

Sold Out

THE THREE COLOMBIANS quickly carried Joseph down the hall to the space leased by the Colombian fashion designer and textile manufacturer Fabricaglobo. Jairo, the apparent ringleader, pulled a syringe from a tote bag and plunged it into Joseph's thigh. "Get me that trunk from the corner," he commanded. The other men dragged the trunk to the center of the room as Jairo lifted Joseph and dropped him inside. Jairo, a big man whose large paunch hung over his belt in an unsightly manner, had a thick black mustache with a perpetual cigar protruding from it. He brushed his hands together, closed the lid, and said, "That oughta hold him 'til we get to the container."

The noise and vibration pounded against Joseph's throbbing head as he regained consciousness. He slid his hands around the dark container confining him, trying in his disoriented state to discern what was happening to him. He judged by the bumping and jerking that he must be in a vehicle, but where and why? His attention was suddenly diverted as he was thrown to the side of the box when the vehicle came to a stop. He heard a truck door slam, and the box was slid a short distance and dropped roughly to the ground. The chattering of voices speaking a foreign language sounded like his abductors were having an argument. The staccato chattering continued as the box was picked up and carried. Joseph's head was aching as he wondered, *Do my brothers hate me enough to do something like this?* Again, the box was dropped, and he heard a loud creaky sound of a heavy metal door opening and then the snapping of the fasteners on the box he was in. The lid opened, and one of the Colombians reached in and pulled him to his feet. He was still bound and gagged the way his brothers had left him. They thrust him to the back of a metal container where he fell against a pile of humanity. Laying against bodies that were crying, moaning, and smelling of sweat and urine, he surmised that the fashion business wasn't the only endeavor of these people. He observed them bringing in cocaine, and now they were practicing the trucker's philosophy of not returning home empty by engaging in human trafficking. Joseph thought, *I must have been a bonus for them. The rest of these poor souls are young girls.*

Several men began carrying boxes into the container and stacking them floor to ceiling in front of the human cargo. The boxes obliterated the light and any possibility of fresh air. Soon they heard the creak and clank of doors closing and then the container wobbled as it was being raised and set upon something. The sound of a diesel engine starting and motion confirmed Joseph's fear that this was not going to end well.

*   *   *

After three days and nights of continuous travel, the truck stopped. The same creaking and clanging of doors opening echoed in Joseph's ears. He felt like he was suffocating under the pungent smell sealed in the container. The space of their prison was so small each person's excrement was smeared on those around them. Soon, the boxes confining the captives were removed, and a wave of fresh air flowed over them.

Men shouting in Spanish began barking orders at them. Joseph was so weak his legs wouldn't move under him. A man grabbed him and tossed him out of the container to the ground. Joseph looked back at the desolate pieces of humanity being carried out of the container and realized that he was better off than most. A glance at his surroundings revealed that they were in some sort of distribution area. Signs on the wall were clearly in Spanish, indiscernible to him. As a worker walked by, Joseph asked, "Are we in Mexico?" For that he received a boot in the face. Three of the twenty-five girls in the container were carried over to the side and thrown in a heap, apparently dead. The rest, including Joseph, were lined up against a wall and hosed down with water. The container was also hosed down, and after they had been given water to drink and some kind of mush to eat, they were herded back into the container, but without the boxes confining them as before.

*   *   *

Another three days over very rough terrain was terribly debilitating on the weakened captives, but Joseph was thankful there was enough space between them to avoid touching one another. On the fourth day, the unloading experience was repeated, only this time, treatment was gentler. The area was in a large walled compound with beautiful Spanish buildings within. It was a fortified area that had armed guards patrolling on top of the walls. The captives were ushered into a shower room, four or five at a time, and ordered to remove all their clothing. Weakness and fatigue had stripped them of any dignity, and they complied without opposition. After they had showered, they were brought to a room containing racks of clothing, and an old Spanish woman selected clothes for each person. From there, they were taken to a hall with long tables and benches. Each person received a cup of water and a small amount of meal. After eating, they were taken to a building best described as barracks and told, through sign language, to pick out a bed and rest.

This routine of washing, eating, and resting continued for over a week until one day, several chauffeured limousines arrived in the compound. The twenty-two remaining girls and Joseph were escorted to an area near one of the gardens outside the main hacienda, and one by one, the girls were escorted past a group of well-dressed men smoking cigars and drinking wine.

After all the girls had been displayed, a man of means, judging by his attire and his air of authority, stepped out and addressed the guests. "My friends, I, Senior Pablo Emilio Escobar Gaviria, raise my glass to you and welcome you to my humble home. It will be your pleasure today to take back with you one or more of New York's finest. My chief assistant, Julio, will be taking your bids, which will be in U.S. dollars and in minimum increments of one thousand."

He nodded to Julio, and the first girl stepped out onto the patio and paraded in front of guests. Performing according to strict instructions beforehand, she stopped, smiled, and slowly twirled. Julio asked, "Who will start the bidding at ten thousand dollars?"

A hand was raised and the bidder said, "Two thousand."

"A very small sum for such a fine specimen," Julio commented. "I have two thousand. Do I see three?"

"Five," came the next bid.

"Very good," replied Julio, and before he could continue, another bid came at ten thousand. "Now we are getting into the spirit," Julio said. "I have ten. Do I hear eleven? I have ten. Give me eleven. Don't let this fine merchandise slip out from you, gentlemen. Give me eleven. Ten going once, ten going twice. Sold to the gentleman for ten thousand dollars."

The remaining girls were auctioned for sums between five thousand and fifteen thousand. At the auctions conclusion, Senior Escobar stepped forward and announced, "We have a special surprise to conclude our auction today. Something all you important men ought to have in your possession. This offering is one of a kind and is so unique that the starting bid will be at least ten thousand dollars." Senior Escobar motioned for Joseph to be brought out.

They had him dressed in a causal silk suit, complete with a Panamanian white hat. Joseph possessed the dark, handsome features of his father, and as such, made a striking impression. He, like the girls before him, had been instructed in their presentation, but he merely stood stoically in front of his pursuers, resenting being sold as a slave.

Senior Escobar continued, "Gentlemen, what we have here is a young man born and bred in the Midwest of America. As has been reported, this area produces some of the finest, smartest, hardest-working people in their country. This lad is of Swiss stock. His great-grandfather, his grandfather, and his father were entrepreneurs. Who among you could not use a handsome manservant intelligent enough to provide you with confident counsel as well."

His sale pitch had the bidders buzzing between them as Escobar asked, "What is the first bid?"

"Ten thousand," one of them shouted.

"Fifteen," came another bid.

"Twenty," shouted another.

"I have twenty thousand dollars," Escobar called out. "Surely you realize I won't allow a prize like this to go for a ridiculous sum as that! Why, some of you paid more than that for some of your horses."

A man in the back slowly rose to his feet. He walked forward and examined Joseph with a keen eye. Then he asked Joseph, "Young man, what do you think will become of you?"

Joseph looked him square in the eye and replied, "I shall one day have you coming to me for favors!"

The entire gathering broke out in laughter over his reply. The man, somewhat shocked at Joseph's reply, stood back, then joining in the laughter, said, "Senior Escobar, I'll give you fifty thousand for this muchacho."

No one seemed willing to counter the man's offer, so Escobar said, "Sold to el Presidente Turbay's minister of security, Carlos Camacho, for fifty thousand dollars.

* * *

When Julio Cesar Turbay Ayala was elected el presidente in 1978, he selected Carlos Camacho as his minister of security. Carlos was born the sixth child of peasant parents. When he was six years old, a man of dubious character, who had close connections to those in the drug trade, abducted him from his parents. The abduction was not for sinister means, but rather, this man took a liking to Carlos and saw great potential in him. He was brought into the man's home and educated in the best schools alongside the man's other children. Later, after receiving a law degree, Carlos engaged in politics and served as a town councilman, was elected to the senate, and then as governor of Cesar.

The man who abducted him had close connections with Pablo Escobar, a Colombian drug lord often referred to as the world's greatest outlaw. He was regarded as the richest and most successful criminal in history. It was from Escobar that Carlos purchased Joseph, and it was his continuing close relationship with a criminal element that cast a cloud over his service for the government. However, the rigors of straddling this precarious and demanding relationship accounted for his need of a reliable manservant.

Carlos brought Joseph to his hacienda and placed him in the hands of a tutor to educate him in the language and in the duties of the household. Joseph was a quick study and performed his duties above expectation. Carlos was not a God-fearing man, but he noticed that Joseph spent much time praying to his God, and he noticed that whatever task he assigned to Joseph, he did it well. As time went on, Carlos continued to delegate more responsibilities to him, and in each area, Joseph prospered until Carlos felt confident in giving him control over the entire household. Of course, Joseph's efficiency also meant that Carlos prospered. When Carlos discovered that Joseph had an aptitude for business, he began handing him portions of his financial dealings until Joseph gained full control over Carlos' investments.

The Lord continued to bless Joseph and, by proxy, Carlos as well. Joseph had become a trusted confidant, a loyal and reliable advisor to Carlos; however, because he was an illegally purchased servant, he was not allowed off the Camacho estate unless accompanied by Carlos and his bodyguards.

Carlos, was now an elderly man. After his first wife died, he had married a much younger woman. She was very beautiful, and Carlos showered her with all the trappings of wealth. He provided her with servants, automobiles, designer clothes, and the finest entertainment; however, the discrepancy in their ages left her unfulfilled.

Now Joseph was well built and handsome. He was tall, had his father's dark chiseled features, and eyes that with a glance could melt a heart. These attributes did not escape the notice of Carlos' wife, and one day, as Joseph was tending to his duties, she approached Joseph in an improperly seductive manner and said, "Come to bed with me!"

Taken back by such a forward advance, Joseph replied, "Señora, your husband has placed me in charge of everything he owns. He doesn't have to concern himself with anything because he has entrusted it to my care. You are the only one who is not under my authority. So I ask you, how could I betray such a trust? It would be a sin against God."

His answer caught her off guard. Feigning an insult, she threw up her nose at his rebuff and said, "My, for a servant bought and paid for, you certainly have a high opinion of yourself."

For a time, she left him to his work, but in the following days, she pursued him relentlessly, using his argument that she was not under his control and twisting it to mean he was under hers. Joseph desperately tried to distance himself from her, but one day, when he went to attend to his duties – as it happened, no one else was around at the time – she came and grabbed him by the sleeve, demanding, "Sleep with me!" He tore himself away, but as he did, his shirtsleeve ripped, and she was left holding it as he fled the house.

She began screaming; and when the other servants came running to see what had happened, she was crying hysterically. "My husband brought this American into our house, and now he thinks he can do anything he pleases," she sobbed. He tried to rape me, but ran off when I screamed. See here, I tore his shirt trying to fight him!"

Some of the servants tried to comfort her while others went to alert her husband. When Carlos arrived, she held up the torn fabric and, with great theatrics, retold the story. Her husband was furious that someone who he had trusted would betray him in such a personal way. Joseph did not receive the benefit of an explanation or a trial and because of his high position; Carlos had Joseph shackled with chains and thrown into prison. It was the place where political prisoners were confined.

CHAPTER 15

Redemption!

AND SO IT was, without formal charges, without an investigation, without a trial, Joseph was a convict. The prison was old, constructed of sun-dried brick during the time of Spanish occupation. It was designed to hold five hundred inmates, today, twice that many were incarcerated. Prison life, with the exception of being confined, was much the same as civilian life. Some prisoners had money and were able to purchase private cells. Others obtained favors by force or by being adept at influencing the right people. Corruption was as prevalent in the prison as it was in the rest of their society, and corruption didn't only exist between prisoners, the officials participated as well. There were the "haves and the have nots," the "honest and the dishonest," just like on the outside.

Joseph had no money. He was delivered to prison with only the clothes he was wearing and left in the courtyard bound in chains, but the Lord was with him. The warden's balcony overlooked the courtyard, and each afternoon, he stepped out on the balcony for his afternoon cigar. On the day that Joseph was dropped at the prison, the warden stepped out for his customary smoke and noticed a man lying in the dirt. The hot sun was beating down on the helpless body, and the warden took pity on him. He called the captain of the guard, had the chains removed, and ordered him to be billeted under a portico. The next day, when the warden was making his rounds, he passed by the portico. Joseph bowed and said, "God will reward you for your kindness, sir."

A few weeks passed, and one day, the warden noticed that Joseph was not in his usual place. He called on the captain of the guard and asked Joseph's whereabouts. "Oh, that one sir, he's a smart one he is. He has become the head cacique."[6]

"No, you must be kidding," The warden replied in surprise. "How could such a newcomer rise to that level so fast?" Intrigued by this unusual ascent, he had Joseph brought before him.

"Your name is Joseph, isn't it?" the warden said, looking at papers spread before him.

"Yes, sir," he answered.

"Where are you from Joseph?"

"Wisconsin, sir."

"Where?"

"Wisconsin, near Canada in America, sir."

"Oh. And how did you manage to end up in my little community?"

"I was kidnapped in New York and brought to Colombia and eventually purchased by Carlos Camacho. In his charge, I was overseer of his household and all of his business interests."

"Tell me, Joseph, how did a slave boy gain such a position?"

"I come from a family of hardworking, honest, entrepreneurs. My father has a national fashion company."

"Really?" the warden said as he rubbed his hand across his mustache, a habit signifying he was thinking. "Joseph," the warden continued, "I'm going to assign you to my office to help with some of my administrative duties."

---

[6] Cacique (ka se'ek): Leader, sometime political, in this instance, prisoner boss

It wasn't long before Joseph proved his worth, and slowly, the warden delegated a major share of his work to him. It was as if God put his hand on everything Joseph did to help him succeed.

*   *   *

Sometime later, the chief usher[7] to the president, Felipe, and the head chef to President Turlay were found guilty of betrayal to the office of the president by providing the press with private and confidential details surrounding the personal life of the president and his family. Both were banished from the household and placed in the custody of the warden at the same prison where Joseph was confined. The warden assigned both of them to be under Joseph's supervision.

They were assigned to the rock pile, a hard, laborious job of smashing rocks, which were then used to build roadbeds. The work was particularly difficult for men who were accustomed to a more sedentary lifestyle. After they had been in custody for a several months, the stress of confinement and the tedious work began to take its toll. They grew restless and irritable. One night, they each had a disturbing dream. When Joseph came the next morning to assign them their daily tasks, he observed that they appeared troubled. "What's the matter with you two, you look like something the cat dragged in?" Joseph remarked.

The usher replied, "We both have had a horrendous dream last night that left us troubled."

Joseph, remembering his own dreams from years before, replied, "You know, some dreams reveal deep meanings. Tell me, what was your dream about?"

---

[7]   USHER: The person with the most important job on the household staff is the chief usher. The chief usher is the head of the household staff. His many responsibilities include working on the household budget and supervising the rest of the staff. The chief usher also coordinates with many other agencies that keep the president's day running smoothly.

So Felipe told Joseph his dream. He said, "It probably doesn't mean anything. It is really weird, but in the dream, I saw a vine grow out of the ground. It grew fast, and it was huge. The vine had three branches, and after it blossomed, it ripened into grapes right before my eyes. I was standing with a cup in my hand, squeezing grapes into a cup, and I gave the juice to His Excellency, the president."

Joseph was listening very intently and praying for God to give him the meaning. After Felipe finished his story, Joseph slowly lifted his head and looked directly into Felipe's eyes. "Here is what your dream means: The three branches are three days. Within three days, President Turley will discover that you had no part in the breach of confidence and will restore you to your former position."

Felipe was ecstatic and said, "Oh, Mr. Joseph, do you really think I can get out of here?"

"It's not for me to say, but I believe that is what God has decided. Felipe, I have treated you fairly since you have been here, haven't I?

"Oh yes, sir, very fairly, even though I detest the work."

"Then please, when you get out of here, remember me and plead my innocence before the president for I have been imprisoned without being charged and without a trial. Will you tell someone of influence about me?"

Felipe, with a wide grin, said, "Sir, how could I forget you?"

When the head chef saw that Joseph had given a favorable interpretation, he said, "Hey, I had a dream too. What does mine mean?"

"How should I know?" Joseph replied, somewhat irritated with the gruff manner of the man. "I haven't even heard it."

"Well, here it is. I had three baskets of bread on my head. In the top basket were all kinds of baked goods for the president's table, but a flock of birds came and were eating all the bread. I tried, but as hard as I tried to swat them away, they came right back."

Joseph's face turned ashen as the true meaning of the dream was revealed to him. He cleared his throat and spoke this to the head chef: "I'll tell you what it means if you really want to know."

"Yes, of course I want to know. Tell me."

"Very good then, here is what it means," Joseph began. "The three baskets are three days. Within three days . . ." Joseph hesitated for a moment.

"Go on," urged the chef.

"All right. Your dream means that within three days, President Turlay will have you beheaded for your deception and will hang you on a tree where the birds will eat your flesh."

The head chef scoffed at the very idea and went away, saying, "This fellow is either a good storyteller or loco in the head."

*   *   *

The presidential palace was buzzing with activity. A feast was being prepared for the president's birthday, and the entire staff was invited. A few hours before the festivities were to begin, the head of the secret service came to the president with news.

"What is it, Emmanuel?" President Turlay asked.

"We have good news, Mr. President. Please look at this report."

The president paged through the papers and at one point raised his eyebrows and said, "Ah ha!" He quickly wrote a response and handed it to Emmanuel. "Now let's go to my party," he said to the others present.

Gaiety, food, and drink prevailed throughout the banquet hall as best wishes were given to the president through song and words. At the conclusion of the evening, the president stood before his well-wishers and made an announcement.

"Friends, I want to thank you for all the support and greetings you have made tonight. Before departing, I would like to relay the results of an investigation my secret service presented to me a short time ago. As you know, a breach of confidentiality was discovered within my household staff some time ago. The results of this act of treason caused my family a great deal of embarrassment."

He waved his hand toward the agent standing behind him, signaling to bring the chief usher and the head chef forward.

"These two men," the president began, "were charged with selling secret information against my family and sent to prison. It has come to my attention that a great injustice has been done.

Apparently, my usher, Felipe, was falsely implicated in this offense." He turned toward Felipe and said, "Sir, if you will forgive this unwarranted intrusion to your life, I would like to reinstall you to your former position."

Relief covered Felipe's face for until that moment, he was not sure why he was being called before the president, especially at his birthday celebration. "Yes, sir," he replied. "It would be my honor." Applause filled the hall as the president shook his hand.

The president turned his attention to the head chef and said, "You are also in this report." The president held up the papers and was silent for several moments, creating an atmosphere of suspense. This report clearly indicates that you alone betrayed me, and further, you had the audacity to falsely implicate a loyal member of my staff. For this offense, you shall lose your head, and as a sign to any who might consider perpetrating such dishonor in the future, I order your body to be hung from a tree outside the central park for all to see."

This took place three days after Joseph's interpretation. However, Felipe did not remember his promise to Joseph when he was restored to his position.

*   *   *

Two full years passed since Felipe was pardoned. He was engaged in serving the president who had just returned from a conference of South American countries. The president was in a particularly ugly mood because several of his contemporaries had criticized him severally for his handling of the labor and student unrest in Colombia and for the guerrilla violence the unrest perpetrated. Leaders of the surrounding countries called him weak and lacking in decisive leadership because he exercised restraint over the protestors. They were concerned that the protests and violence would spread to their countries if not dealt with firmly.

The president sat alone in his bedroom, sipping on a glass of wine before going to bed. During the night, he became restless and began dreaming.

In the dream, he was standing on the banks of the Orinoco River, and seven fat, well-nourished cows were grazing on the lush grass of the riverbanks.

As they were peacefully feeding, seven huge, ugly cows with long horns emerged from the river, attacked and killed the fat cows.

The violence of the attack disturbed him so that he awoke, got up, and called for a glass of milk, hopefully to calm his nerves. He returned to bed and fell asleep, but began dreaming again.

This time, a stalk of grain grew up before him, and on the stalk, there were seven heads of grain, healthy and good.

Next to them, another stalk grew up with seven heads of grain, thin and diseased. The diseased grain infected the healthy heads and caused them to die.

He awoke with a mind so troubled he had his usher, Felipe, summon Monsignor Alejandro. After retelling his dreams, he asked the priest to relate it's meaning, but the monsignor was unable to do so.

Felipe, who was also present, suddenly had a thought. "Mr. President, this has caused me to remember a time when I was falsely accused of betrayal and imprisoned. Sir, while in prison, the head chef, who was also imprisoned, and I each had a dream on the same night. We were also distressed over their meaning, but it just so happened there was a young American, who was also imprisoned and was serving as an attendant to the warden. This American interpreted our dreams, and things turned out exactly as he interpreted. I was reinstated to my position, and the head chef was executed. This American told us this would happen in three days, and it was three days later at your birthday party that the interpretation came true."

The president, visibly upset and eager for relief, sent for Joseph to be brought from the prison. When Joseph was showered, shaved, and properly clothed, he came before the president. "Young man," the president said to Joseph, "I had two dreams last night that for some odd reason have greatly upset me. No one on my staff, including the monsignor, can tell me their meaning, but I have heard that you have that ability. Is that true?"

"No, sir, I don't have the ability. It isn't me, Mr. President, but for reasons I don't understand, God sometimes gives the meaning to me."

"Well, let's get with it then and see if God decides to tell you what has caused me this distress." Then the president related both dreams to Joseph.

After listening to the retelling of the dreams, Joseph bowed his head and silently prayed. When he finished, he looked directly at the president and said, "Mr. President, both of your dreams have the same meaning. God is revealing to you what is going to take place in your country over the next fourteen years."

This had the president's attention, for he said, "Tell me, what it is that has God so concerned?" The president was not a very religious man, but he did have respect for God.

"The seven fat cows and the seven good heads of grain represent the next seven years in Colombia. They will be years of prosperity and peace, but during those seven years, a great evil will weave its way into the culture. The country's administrators and the people will become complacent and allow this evil to infiltrate from the lowest to the highest. The Colombian leaders will ignore God and allow graft and corruption to flourish."

"What about the ugly cows and the diseased grain? How do they fit in?" the president asked with eagerness.

The seven huge, ugly cows and the seven diseased heads of gain represent seven years of violence, corruption, and immoral activities like nothing you could imagine. This will come about as a result of dishonoring God and Christ. Thieves and drug cartels will ravage the country. Colombia's leaders will be repugnant in the eyes of other nations because of this lawlessness, and you, Mr. President, will be stripped of office and humiliated."

President Turlay sat back in his chair with a look of utter despair over the interpretation. "What are we to do? What are we to do?" he kept asking.

"Mr. President," Joseph answered, "May I make a suggestion?"

"Yes, of course, go right ahead."

"You must look for a discerning and wise man, someone above reproach who has never benefited from ill-gotten gains, and place him as administrator over major government policies and personnel selection. He must have unquestioned power in these areas, within the constitution, in order to build a cadre of strong, principled people at all levels of the government, who place honor and freedom above personal risk and danger."

President Turlay looked toward his cabinet advisors, who were all nodding affirmatively at Joseph's suggestions, and he asked them, "How can we find anyone such as this, someone so fearless?"

The president's chief of staff spoke up and said, "Mr. President, I think we already have!"

Again, the cabinet members murmured agreement, so President Turlay turned to Joseph and said, "You, you shall be the one. I have met no one that has such discernment and wisdom. You were not afraid to stand firm and tell me of my fate. Since you say God has made all this known to you, it must be in His plan to have you continue in its application. I am going to place you under myself, as second in authority, to seek out and destroy all corrupt officials and to punish the guilty to the fullest extent of our law."

*   *   *

A proclamation was issued by the president, stating that Joseph would be known as chief administrator of Colombia, reporting only to the president. In addition to this authority, President Turlay provided him with a fine wardrobe, a beautiful secure home, a detail of guards and servants to attend to his needs. It was at this time the president's daughter, Diana, caught Joseph's eye, and later his heart, which in due time provided him with a family.

Joseph was thirty years old when he entered President Turlay's service. He traveled throughout Colombia, appointing new officials in many communities and encouraging those who were upright with additional support. His method of personnel selection was simple – he prayed – often, sometimes all night, seeking the wisdom and discernment from God to carry out the task he was given.

However, his enemies continued to grow stronger and increasingly more violent. Time after time, after installing a new police chief or mayor, the drug lords would kidnap a family member and threaten to kill them if authorities disrupted their drug and human trafficking trade. Joseph finally devised a plan, which called for complete, absolute control of small sections of the country. He called it by the American phrase "Operation Circle the Wagons." He took control of an entire army division and, beginning in the state of Cundinamarca, the state where the capital city of Bogota was located, purged the area of drug cartels and dishonest administrators.

In each area, he left loyal troops behind to maintain peace and prevent gangs and dishonest civilians from reentering. Honest judges were sworn in to rebuild respect for the law and missionaries were invited to establish churches that would bring the good news of the gospel to the Colombian people.

Before the end of the first seven years, Joseph married Diana, and they had two sons. The oldest he named Masses, after his great-grandfather, and the youngest he named Zachary, after his grandfather.

*   *   *

Relative peace was attained during the first seven years under Joseph's management. Relative compared to the years before "Operation Circle the Wagons" began. Northern Colombia was purged of lawlessness and security forces set in place by Joseph guarded the areas from criminal infiltration. There were, however, southern areas under control of the cartels. The brutal methods of these criminal elements forced victims to flee to the north to escape the violence and corruption.

Refugee's flooded northern cities pleading for help from the government. President Turlay's response was "Go to Joseph and do what he tells you to do."

Joseph renovated an abandoned factory, turning it into a barracks, housing the displaced Colombians. He personally met with them and explained his concern for their welfare and his plan to overtake the criminals and return them to their homes. He gained their hearts by his loving concern, and many of the young men volunteered to join in his operation. Armed with this influx of trainees, he intensified his efforts and captured or killed thousands of the cartels forces. The ones who escaped were driven out of Colombia to neighboring countries.

As "Operation Circle the Wagons" succeeded, Colombia became a safer, more prosperous place to reside. Families gathered together once more, festivals were held in villages, towns, and cities; Colombia began to attract foreign businesses, and the tourist trade flourished.

CHAPTER 16

The Ultimatum

THINGS WERE CHANGING in the U.S. as well. It was becoming increasingly difficult to compete with the garment and fashion industry of the third world countries. They were achieving great strides in innovation and marketing while having the advantage of low-labor cost. The U.S. in contrast was experiencing just the opposite. The higher standard of living and union labor pushed production costs beyond the competitive edge, and this comfort level of the U.S. workforce also developed an attitude of complacency, which diminished the human quest for greatness, thus limiting innovation.

Zurbriggen Classic Wear was among the companies experiencing this competitive pressure. Thomas and Rob had been discussing possible solutions to overcome their sales decline and had made a decision. Thomas called a meeting of their sons to inform them of their plan to combat this problem.

"Boys," he began, "you are the generation that will be called on to carry this company forward. It should come as no surprise that time has a way of changing the way things must be done. When that happens, a company either gets out in front or is trampled by those coming from behind. Colombia's fashion industry is being noticed around the world for their high-quality and exotic ideas. The city of Medellin has become South America's clothing center. Inexmoda, a Colombian nonprofit organization, researches fashion concepts and provides special training to educate the Colombian textile industry in an effort to help them excel in the world marketplace. To this end, they organize a worldwide fashion tradeshow every year in Medellin. We are going to send all of you to Medellin each with a separate assignment. We want you to diagnose the new styles, the production methods, and explore the possibility of having some of our production transferred to Colombian facilities. Rob will give you your assignments and make travel arrangements. Any questions?"

Simon spoke up and asked, "Why are you sending all of us?"

"There are several garment factories in Colombia," Rob replied. "All of them will be represented at this show. We want to see just how competitive they can be among themselves, and there isn't enough time during the show for one or two of you to contact all of them. All of you will be going except Benjamin. He will remain behind."

*   *   *

The entourage from Zurbriggen Classic Wear arrived in Medellin and proceeded to undertake their assigned tasks. Lingering in their minds as motivation to tend to business was the catastrophe of their actions at the New York show years before.

Each of the men did their due diligence and gathered the information that their father's wanted. It was at the finale of the show that the unexpected happened. Just as the trumpets sounded to announce the Best of the Class winner, gunshots rang out filling the auditorium with ear-piercing blasts. Instinctively, scores of attendees dropped to the floor as gunmen appeared on all the balconies. Over the PA system came a voice demanding, "¡Tranquilo – tranquilo digo! Cálmese y no harán daño a nadie." (Quiet – quiet I say! Quiet down and no one will be hurt.)

A hush fell over the room except for the fearful whimpering of several women. Then the voice over the loudspeakers continued, "I am Pablo Escobar, leader of the Medellin drug Cartel. This is my city. Colombia is my country. I, and I alone, am the one the people of Colombia should look to for protection, not this weasel of a president or his chief administrator lackey.

Today we are sending a message for all Colombia. We will not tolerate the disruption of our business anymore. We will be striking back forcefully against this government intrusion starting with fifty of you as hostages. Here's a message to the Colombian leaders. This is just the beginning. If you want these people returned, pull back your troops and cease this military invasion of our territory, or there will be more to follow!"

Signaling to his men, he said, "Round them up and take them to the truck." The gunmen spilled onto the center's floor, grabbing, pushing, and assaulting anyone who did not comply. A semitrailer was backed up to the stage door, and fifty attendees were loaded in the trailer, among those taken prisoner were the sons of Thomas Zurbriggen and Rob Buchanan.

Outside of the center, guarded by armored trucks and pickups with machine guns mounted in their beds, the semi disappeared down a city street. They were only a two blocks away when the police and army set up a roadblock with their vehicles. Escobar's armored vehicles sped directly toward the roadblock, sending a hail of bullets toward the military. As they approached the blockage, Escobar's men fired a grenade launcher toward the cars and drove the armored trucks into them, leaving a hole for the semi to drive through. The police and the military were forced to hold their fire for fear of killing the civilians.

Ten blocks farther, some of the assailants' armored vehicles and four armed pickups fell back to create a line of defense against the pursuing military as the semi and its armed escort sped out of the city. The army surrounded Escobar's defense force and destroyed all that had stayed behind. However, the kidnapped victims, who Escobar planned to use as pawns in his power play, were whisked away to parts unknown.

*   *   *

Forty minutes after the abduction, the semi pulled off on a
remote jungle road and turned on a trail barely wide enough
to allow passage. The kidnappers opened the rear doors of the
semitrailer and ordered the hostages out. The hostage's hands were
bound together, and they were blindfolded before being loading
into five vans that had made a timely coordinated arrival. Each
van was driven to a different destination far into the bowels of the
Colombian jungle. Daniel, Nathan, and their cousins were altogether
in one van with no idea of where they were going or what would
become of them.

Several hours later, the van with the Zurbriggen captives
stopped. A chorus of Spanish-speaking voices, all talking over one
another, replaced the monotonous drone of the van. The young
men were pulled from the vehicle, dragged to a cage, and thrown
inside. As the Spanish voices faded away, Daniel was the first to
speak.

"Are we all here?" he asked as he called out each of their names.

"Good, at least we're together. Rueben, use your teeth to pull off
my blindfold."

Rueben maneuvered in position, found the back of the cloth
covering Daniel's eyes, and pulled it over his head. He in turn did
the same thing for Rueben. They looked around to see if they were
guarded but saw no one.

"Okay, Rueben, let's see if we can loosen the ropes on our
brothers." Within a few minutes, they had freed the bindings on two
of the others. Now they had hands to work with. When all were free
of restraints, they began to appraise in their situation. They were in
a cage made from tree limbs tied together to form a crude jail cell.

"We ought to be able to loosen these knots," Nathan said as he
observed their confinement cage.

Simon sat with his back against the cage, tears streaming down
his face, as he whimpered, "This is what we get!"

"What are you moaning about?" Nathan snapped.

"We're getting what's coming to us for what we did to Joseph, that's what I mean!"

"Having a pity party isn't going to get us out of here. Let's see if we can untie one of these knots."

"How about thinking this through first," Rueben suggested. "We have no idea where we are. If we were to get out, chances are we would die in the jungle before being found."

"I think Rueben is right," Dan said in agreement. They didn't put us in a cage that invites escape if it wasn't part of a well-thought-out plan."

Simon joined in and said, "My gut tells me our captors don't need to guard us closely because there is no place to escape to. This was a well-orchestrated siege of a public place. Taking fifty people and separating us means we are going to be used as barter for something."

As they were trying to make sense of their dilemma, a fat Colombian with a movie camera in hand strolled over to the cage and said in broken English, "Eh Gringos, you's got loose, si? Maybe usted ha make a imagen de la pelicula para me. Hey, tu, ya con, with the little bebe lagrimas en sus eyes. Give me a mucho smile. Usted ser on television."

Simon, feeling emotionally distraught and now being humiliated by this Neanderthal, spat back, "You fat coward. The only thing separating you from a good beating are these bars. Open this cage and you'll be begging for mercy."

"Ooh ooh, the pocp gringo cries like bambino. Here, bambino, call a su mama, and we get you pezon to suck."

"The name's Buchanan, Simon Buchanan, and you are goin' ta eat those words, whatever they mean!"

The fat man threw back his head and laughed as he shoved a plate filled with tortillas under the door.

Simon, more suspicious than sensible, said, "You don't suppose they would poison us, do you?"

Rueben frowned at his paranoia and said, "Ya, they pulled off this caper and are hiding us out in the jungle just so they could poison us."

* * *

Havoc reigned in Medellin that afternoon. The police, the mayor, and social organizations were doing all they could to assure the remaining visitors that no harm would come to them. The local politicians were frantic that this adverse notoriety would deter tourism and other trade-show events, all of which filled the coffers of the local bureaucracy.

The army found two of the attackers alive in the rubble and interrogated them for information. All they learned was what they had surmised; Pablo Escobar was making a direct challenge against the government for control, and power was his opiate. On one occasion in the past, he attempted to buy his way into Colombian politics by offering to pay off the nation's $10 billion national debt. Joseph's effort to rid the country of the criminal element had put a dent in his enterprises. Unsuccessful at buying his power, he was now determined to take it by force.

President Turlay called his cabinet together and asked Joseph to attend. "Gentlemen," the president was nearly shouting as he entered the room, "we have a situation. I'm sure all of you have heard of Escobar's demands. My question to you is how are we going to solve it?"

One of the men spoke up and said, "Mr. President, even if we knew where the captives were located, we would risk all or many of their lives by a rescue attempt."

Another said, "Keeping to our no-negotiating-with-terrorists policy would most likely result in the death of all of them."

President Turlay interjected, "Either course of action would result in a horrific public relations fiasco."

Just then, the president's secretary ran into the room, shouting, "Mr. President, quick, turn on the television."

One of the men opened the cabinet at the end of the room and turned the television on. A news bulletin alert was flashing across the screen, interrupting regular programing.

A reporter appeared and said, "We have breaking news. This is Luis Fernando reporting. As you may be aware, gunmen raided the closing exercises of the International Fashion Show being held in our city's civic center and escaped with fifty hostages. Our station has just received a film sent by Pablo Escobar, the apparent perpetrator of this abduction. It is of poor quality, so pay close attention."

A home-style movie began to play, showing the caged Buchanan and Zurbriggen men and featured the narrative of Simon Buchanan. After it finished, Pablo Escobar appeared saying, "This is Pablo Escobar. Be calm, el Presidente, all will be well if you follow these instructions: Remove the chief administrator from his position and abolish your failed indoctrination program.

"Do this, and all the people will be returned unharmed. Failure to follow my directions will result in the killing of one hostage every hour, and their body thrown in the street. Any attempt at rescue will result in two deaths each hour. It would be futile to try a rescue since the hostages have been separated and are being held in several locations. You have until nine o'clock tomorrow morning to make your decision or the sacrifice will begin."

"This note was delivered to our studio approximately thirty minutes ago. It is regarding the hostage taking at our civic center. When we have more details, we will report on them immediately. This has been Luis Fernando reporting. We now return to our regular programming."

A deafening quiet invaded the situation room after the television was turned off. None of the president's men knew what to do. The president turned to Joseph and asked, "Son, are you all right? You're as white as a ghost."

Joseph stroked the side of his face before replying, "I, ah, oh, I'm fine."

However, he wasn't fine, for he recognized that the men in the cage were his brothers.

"Our time is limited," the president continued. "Do you have you any ideas, Joseph?"

Joseph regained his composure and replied, "I have a thought, but I don't think you will like it Mr. President."

"Don't worry about what I like or don't like, we have a crisis on our hands that is begging for an answer."

"Sir, if you remember, you summoned me directly from prison."

"Of course, I remember. What has that to do with this situation?"

"Mr. President, do you know who placed me in prison?"

"No, I never inquired."

"It was your minister of security, Carlos Camacho. He bought me at a slave auction that was held at the home of his good friend, Pablo Escobar."

The president's eyebrows shot up at that revelation, and he challenged Joseph, "Are you positive? Carlos has been in my service for many years."

"Sir, I am sorry to be the one to tell you, but I handled all of Senior Camacho's affairs until I was falsely accused of impropriety. His motive for public service is not patriotic. It was to be a conduit of inside information for Escobar, and for that he was generously compensated. I know this for a fact because I kept his books."

"This is distressing, Joseph, but what has this to do with the kidnappers?"

"It is just a thought, sir, but I was thinking that someone who has a close personal relationship to Escobar might be in a position to provide us with valuable information."

The president jumped from his chair and said, "You may be on to something, Joseph," and he rang for his secretary. "Summon my minister of security and have him escorted to the situation room immediately," he ordered.

* * *

Due to the lateness of the hour, it took some time to locate Carlos Camacho. He was dining at a small obscure restaurant on the outskirts of the city when his own security force came and notified him that the president requested his presence.

When he entered the situation room, anxiety was spread across his face. "What is it, Mr. President, that required this urgency?"

"Take a seat, Carlos," the president said in a stern voice.

Carlos sat down and nervously eyed Joseph in the corner.

"You know the men of my cabinet, and I understand that you are intimately acquainted with my chief administrator."

He shook his head affirmatively and looked away.

"Carlos, it has come to my attention that you and Escobar are good friends! A rather strange camaraderie for my minister of security, wouldn't you say?"

Angrily, Carlos shot back, "Who told you that, this American?" as he spit out American with distain.

"I've ordered a full investigation of your household, Carlos. My finance department is probably at your door as we speak, but that's another subject. We have a terrorist threatening the lives of our foreign friends and wreaking havoc on our country. Now I'll tell you why you're here. You are going to take me to Escobar's family."

"Mr. President, I have met this Escobar, but I know nothing of his whereabouts."

"I don't believe a word of what you say, Camacho, but it would be in your best interest to refresh your memory." The president waved his hand, indicating for the door to be opened. Outside in the corridor, Camacho's wife, his adult children, and his grandchildren were paraded past, allowing Carlos to see the procession.

"Here's the deal, Carlos, your family is going to be held under arrest. For every hostage Escobar kills, a member of your family will be sentenced to life in prison. Now does that do anything to improve your memory?"

"Mr. President, I've known you to be a kind, gentle man. Surely you are not serious."

"Oh, I'm very serious. The only way to deal with a criminal like Escobar is to take what he values most. The fact that you have been feeding from his trough, Mr. Camacho, makes you a contributor to the havoc his has created.

Carlos buried his head in his hands as tears dropped to the carpet.

"I don't know where he is or anything about this terrible mess."

"You do know where his family is, don't you?"

Carlos hesitated for a moment and then said, "Yes, I believe I do."

"Listen, Carlos, if we are able to detain his family, yours will be set free."

Carlos quickly grabbed a piece of paper, wrote down directions to Escobar's hacienda, and gave specific instructions on the security surrounding his estate.

*   *   *

By five thirty in the morning, the army had overcome Escobar's security force and brought his family to a detention center. Television reporters and camera were brought in, and President Turlay began broadcasting the following:

"My fellow Colombian's – the vicious act of terror perpetrated upon visitors to our country at the National Fashion Trade Show in Medellin two days ago stands as an attack on the freedom of you, the Colombian people. This criminal element is seeking to control our nation. Now they are threatening to murder innocent people if we do not hand over our country to their wicked, unlawful behavior.

"The man leading this corrupt assault is a person who has become immensely wealthy at the expense of the Colombian people. He is a thief and murderer, who has robbed you of peace, prosperity, and the pride of holding your heads high as Colombians. This man is Pablo Escobar. The following is a message from me to Pablo Escobar:

"Mr. Escobar, my forces have raided your compound, and I have ordered fifty members of your family and close associates detained. You have threatened to kill one of the hostages every hour if we did not stop fighting your unlawful drug trafficking and human slave trade business.

"Listen carefully, Pablo Escobar! This is the judgment that you will be bringing down on your very own family. For every one of those innocent people that you harm, I will condemn one of your family members to life in prison!"

As he spoke, the camera closed in on Escobar's family standing off to the side. The president pointed toward one of the little boys and said, "and the first one receiving a life sentence will be this little grandson of yours!

"We Colombians have had enough of your murderous threats. We will never negotiate with tyrants. The fate of your family now rests in your hands.

"Mr. Escobar, for once in your life, make a wise decision!"

CHAPTER 17

Oh, What a Tangled Web We Weave

IT WAS 8:45 a.m. The deadline imposed by Escobar was fifteen minutes away. The president and his cabinet sat in his chambers, waiting anxiously. A loud ticking from the grandfather clock on the other side of the room was the only audible sound. The president looked at his watch; it was 8:55. Waiting, oh, the horrible task of waiting. The clock at the end of the room began striking. It was nine o'clock. The men sat without uttering a word, occasionally casting a nervous glance toward one another. Would the president's ultimatum work, or would it bring down a reign of terror? The gravity of the confrontation even seemed to make their breathing difficult, a natural response, I suppose, to a tense situation. The clock gave a quarter hour strike; it was 9:15, and there was no news of the hostages, good or bad. At ten o'clock, the president stood and addressed his cabinet, "Gentlemen, do not count on victory too soon. I would not be surprised if this evil man would try something desperate to save face. We may not have reason to celebrate just yet."

President Turlay's private secretary hurried into the room and announced, "Mr. President, there's another news bulletin about to be announced." Again, the president's men turned to the television with uncertainty.

"Fellow Colombians, this is Luis Fernando reporting. It seems that our media has become the go-between for President Turlay and Pablo Escobar. Yesterday, we played a message from Mr. Escobar, challenging our president's authority to rid the country of his business activities, only to be followed by the president giving Mr. Escobar an ultimatum, namely, 'If you harm any of the kidnapped hostages, I will incarcerate an equal number of your family for life.' The president vowed to make the four-year-old grandson of Mr. Escobar the first recipient of a life sentence.

"This morning, our janitor discovered a videotape in our mail slot. It is a response from Mr. Escobar to President Turlay. We will play it for you now." A grainy video began to play.

"My fellow Colombians, many of you have benefited from my generosity in the past. I have been able to pass my good fortune on to you because of freedom. Now your president wants to play the role of a gangster, placing my family under arrest and threatening to pass life prison sentences to my family and singling out my little grandson. What kind of country has this become, where an innocent child can be imprisoned for the rest of his life? For what I ask you is this being done?

"I'll tell you about the president's motivation. He has become the laughing stock of all South America. The other leaders have publically called him un cachorro de perro.[8] Amigos, all I want is freedom to engage in commerce. I want freedom from these foreigners who have invaded our country and are stealing the ideas of our most creative citizens. That is why I made a bold gesture at the fashion show. It was to bring attention to the way our president has sold out his own people because he desperately wants the approval of the northern gringos. It was always my intention to set these foreigners free. As long as they were free to leave us Colombians to ourselves. The foreign thieves are being released as we speak. Would the macho hombre we call our president

---

[8]   A puppy dog

please do the same and release my little grandson? Adios for now compañeros.[9] I'm Pablo Escobar, your friend forever!"

President Turlay motioned to turn the TV off. He turned and addressed his cabinet members, "I knew Escobar would do something. I'm only glad it was verbiage vibrato instead of his usual destruction. If the hostages are indeed set free, I want them brought to the president's office for debriefing."

As the weary foreigners entered the capital, Joseph stepped close to the president and whispered in his ear. The president nodded affirmatively and gave instructions to direct the Buchanan and Zurbriggen group to a private room.

Joseph had grown a beard and was more mature in appearance than the boyish figure his family would remember. Still, he desired to prevent them from recognizing him, so he put on a large sombrero that shielded his face, and he entered the room where his family had been sent with Emanuel, a Mexican who was to serve as an interpreter.

"All rise," Emanuel said in a loud voice.

The Zurbriggen family immediately rose and faced Emanuel and Joseph.

Emanuel then said, "Allow me to introduce Colombia's chief administrator, second-in-command to President Turlay. I present the president's chief administrator, Senior José.[10] I will act as his interpreter. He understands English but does not speak it well."

Joseph wanted to question his family without them being aware of his identity.

"He sido informado de que hayan venido aquí para robar información confidencial relativa a nuestra industria de la confección."

Emanuel translated, "I have been informed that you have come here to steal proprietary information relating to our garment industry."

---

[9] Companions
[10] José is Spanish for Joseph.

"No, sir," Rueben answered. "It is true that we came to investigate your garment production, but only for the purpose of deciding if it might be to our mutual benefit to contract some of our production in Colombia. We are the sons of Thomas Zurbriggen and Robert Buchanan of Zurbriggen Classic Wear. We are honest men!"

"Ridículo! Todos ustedes no terminan juntos como 'supuestos rehenes' por accidente. Yo creo que está colaborando con Escobar."

"Ridiculous! All of you did not end up together as 'supposed hostages' by accident. I believe you are collaborating with Escobar," Emanuel translated.

"With respect, sir, that is not true. We are a group of twelve brothers and cousins from Wisconsin. Our youngest is at home, and one brother has died."

Joseph rose from his chair and said, "Creo es espías industriales, pero será elaborar una prueba para buscar la verdad. Deberá seleccionar uno entre vosotros para volver a su casa para traer a su hermano para mí. De esta manera voy a ver si están diciendo la verdad en incluso la más pequeña de las cosas. Mientras tanto, el resto de ustedes seguirá aquí en la cárcel." He turned to Emanuel and said, "Ponerlos bajo custodia durante tres días para decidir si aceptan mi desafío."

Joseph rose from his chair and said, "I believe you are industrial spies, but I will devise a test to seek out the truth. You shall select one from among you to return to your home to bring your younger brother to me. This way I shall see if you are telling the truth in even the smallest of things. Meanwhile, the rest of you will remain here in prison." He turned to Emanuel and said, "Put them in custody for three days to decide if they will accept my challenge."

*　　*　　*

After three days, he had them brought before him again and issued an ultimatum. "He dado este gran pensado. Ya que soy un Dios temeroso a hombre permitiré todos, excepto uno, para volver a su casa. Los restantes uno va ser encarcelados hasta su regreso. Si no regresa su hermano será tratado como un espía y ejecutado. Si vuelve usted debe traer a su hermano con usted para verificar la veracidad de sus palabras. Eso es todo!" And he left them to deliberate.

After three days, he had them brought before him again and issued an ultimatum. "I have given this considerable thought. Since I am a God-fearing man, I will allow all of you, except for one, to return to your home. The one remaining will be incarcerated until your return. If you do not return, your brother will be treated as a spy and executed. If you return, you must bring your younger brother with you to verify the truth of your words. That is all!" And he left them to deliberate.

They gathered around, perplexed over this strange treatment, but saying to one another, "Do you suppose God is punishing us for what we did to our brother?"

Simon admitted, "We saw how distressed he was when we tied him up and threw him in that closet. He pleaded with us, but we were so sick of him we wouldn't listen to his pleas."

Rueben replied, "Didn't I try to stop you? I knew it wasn't right even if he was a spoiled brat. Now we're paying for our stupid mistakes."

Joseph had installed a microphone close to where his brothers and cousins were gathered, and he was in the next room, listening to the entire discourse. Conflicting emotions of love and betrayal surged through him like a roaring river, but now that they were here he was overcome with the loss of his family and the possibility of being reunited.

As this mixture of emotions flooded through him, he broke out in tears. Regaining his composure, he straightened up, wiped his eyes, and returned to face his family. "Enlazar una! Ordenó," he ordered, pointing to Simon. "Ahora estará en camino. Mis hombres te verán." "Bind that one!" he ordered, pointing to Simon. "Now be on your way. My men will see you out."

As they were being escorted to the vehicle that would take them to the airport, Joseph gave his men specific orders. "Place five thousand dollars American currency in each of their wallets and don't return them until they are ready to board the plane. Then give them their wallets, but hand their passports to them separately so they will not have to look for them in their wallets."

It wasn't until they had a layover in Dallas when Simon was going to buy a soft drink that he opened his wallet and saw five thousand dollars in fresh bills. "What is this?" he exclaimed. "This is more money than I came with."

The others looked in their wallets and discovered the same. Rueben's heart sank as he turned to his family and cried, "What has God done to us? We have been tricked, and we most likely will be charged with theft if we go back. Then we will all be imprisoned!"

*   *   *

Upon arriving back in Eau Claire, they quickly gathered with their fathers, Thomas and Rob. Reuben became the spokesman and related all that had happened to them.

"The Chief Administrator José treated us quite harshly and accused us of spying. We told him that we were honest men, that we were brothers and cousins, and we told him all about you, Dad, about the company, and we even told him that one brother was dead, and our youngest was home with you."

Anxious to justify their actions, Nathan blurted out, "José, the administrator, said he was going to test our honesty. The test required Simon to be held in confinement, and we were ordered to return with our younger brother."

"What? Why on this bloomin' earth did you volunteer that you had a younger brother?" Thomas shouted in anger at the thought of losing another son.

"Don't blame Nathan, Dad, the man questioned us closely about our family. We had no way of knowing he would demand Benjamin be brought back."

"That's right," Dan interjected. "Nothing this fellow did made any sense. For instance, why fill our wallets with cash? Is he just playing a game? He must be pulling something, but what?"

Thomas paced the room, saying, "No, no, we've already lost Joseph, now Simon, and you want me to turn Benjamin over to you? It's too much to ask!"

*   *   *

Months passed as Thomas struggled with what to do. One day, as Rob and Thomas were praying, Rob asked, "Thomas, do you think God wants us to send the boys back to Colombia?"

Surprised at the comment, Thomas answered with a question, "Why would you ask the question like that, Rob?"

"It's hard to explain, but we are getting beat-up in the marketplace, and if that's not enough, the union is trying to get our people to join. If that happens, we're out of business, unless . . ."

Thomas could see where this conversation was going. "No, Rob, I am not sending our boys down to that drug infested rat hole again."

"I've heard they made great progress in forcing the cartels out. I wasn't trying to be flippant about God wanting to send them back. I just know that God sometimes does things that appear stupid to us but, in the end, works it all out if we trust Him."

"You're right about one thing, Rob. It sounds like a stupid idea!"

"Listen, Thomas, you and I both know that we will never have a moment's piece until we at least try to get Simon back. It would be just like our God to use something like our business to prod us into action. If you will remember, our main reason for going there in the first place was to evaluate the possibility of having our products made in their factories."

"Call the boys in. We'll have a talk."

As the family gathered together, Rob relayed the conversation he and Thomas had that morning. Jude responded by saying, "But that man, José, warned us that he would not see us again unless our little brother is with us. Dad, if you will send Benjamin with us, we will go. If you will not, then only a fool would willingly walk to his death."

Jude stood before his father and vowed, "Send Benjamin with me. You can hold me personally responsible for him. If I do not bring him back, I'll bear the blame for the rest of my life! As it is, we could have been there and back twice if we had not delayed."

His father, Rob, and his uncle, Thomas, looked at one another, nodded, and Thomas said, "You're right. Prepare to make the trip, but take gifts along for José, the administrator. Include some of Zurbriggen's finest products and include things from our state such as cheese and honey."

Rob added, "And take back the money that was placed in your wallets. It may have been a test for honesty."

"Gather round, boys," Thomas said, "I want to ask for God's direction. Dear Heavenly Father, we bow before you, humbly asking for your protection, wisdom, and guidance. Please, Lord, protect all of our boys, and, God Almighty, grant mercy from the Colombian man so that he will release Simon and Benjamin. Lord, as for me, I accept your will. If I am to grieve, I will grieve, but oh my Lord, losing another son would be the death of me. Amen."

CHAPTER 18

The Revealing

PASSAGE WAS BOOKED to Colombia. The gifts Thomas recommended were packed, and they made their way to the Colombian capital to present themselves to the chief administrator. When they arrived, Joseph was informed that the Americans had returned and were asking for an audience with him. "Did they bring the younger brother with them?" he asked.

"Si, Senior José, they have the niño," his steward replied.

"Good. Take them to my house and prepare a dinner. They are to eat with me at noon."

The steward did as Joseph directed, but again, the men were confused and frightened. They thought, "We were probably brought here because of the money that was in our wallets. He will not only accuse us of being spies, but also thieves."

Levy said, "He'll probably make us slaves. They do that in these third world countries, ya know!"

So they went up to Joseph's steward. As they were about to enter the house, Rueben said, "Please, sir, could you clear up some of our confusion? When we left here last time, we had a layover at the Dallas Airport. It was then that we discovered each of us had five thousand dollars in our wallets that were not ours. We don't know how it got there, so we have brought it back with us."

"It's all right, senior, don't be afraid. I was told that the one true God of Heaven has given you this treasure." Then he brought Simon out to them. They descended on Simon with cheers, lifting him on their shoulders and marching around the compound. After the celebration settled down, they were full of questions about his treatment and if he had gained any idea as to the purpose of these strange requests. He told them he was treated well, fed well, but had no contact with José since they left. The steward took them in the house and directed them to a washroom so they could refresh themselves. They unpacked their gifts and displayed them nicely on the veranda because they were told they were going to eat there with José.

When Joseph arrived, they presented their gifts to him, bowing to him out of fear as if he were royalty.

"¿Cómo has estado? Tomó usted mucho tiempo para volve. ¿Cómo su padre, son todavía viven?" Joseph commented.

"How have you been? It took you a long time to return. How are your father's? Are they still living?" the steward interpreted.

They bowed low and nervously replied, "They are well but somewhat distressed because all of their offspring are in a foreign country, and they are concerned about our safe return."

As he looked them over, he saw his brother Benjamin peeking from behind one of the older brothers.

"¿Es este su hermano más joven, que me dijiste sobre?"

"Is this your youngest brother, the one you told me about?"

"Yes, he is," they said, pushing Benjamin out in front.

The sight of his little brother gripped Joseph's innermost emotions. He looked at Benjamin and said, "Dios ser misericordioso a usted, hijo mío" (God be gracious to you, my son), and he hurriedly left the room so they could not see tears welling up in his eyes. He went to a private room, washed his face to gain control, then returned to dining room and said, "Servir la comida." (Serve the food.) Joseph sat by himself and the brothers by themselves. They were seated from the youngest to the oldest facing Joseph. This behavior astonished them, but they were in a foreign country and were hoping that this visit would end well.

* * *

After dinner, Joseph told them they should relax and enjoy the evening as his guest. He told them through his interpreter that in the morning, they would be free to make contacts with any in the garment industry that they preferred. After dismissing them, he gave instructions to his house steward, "When you take their luggage to the car in the morning, pay close attention to which suitcase belongs to the youngest." He handed the steward the signet ring the president gave him at his installation ceremony.

"Diego, I want you to place this ring in the youngster's bag without being detected." And the steward did as he was told.

The next morning, a car arrived, and the men were told they could use it to visit the industrial sites. The steward loaded their luggage in the car and bid them goodbye. About thirty minutes after they had left, Joseph instructed his steward to take some security men and stop them. "When you catch them, say, 'Is this the way you repay hospitality by stealing the administrator's ring?'"

When they caught up with the men, they did just as instructed, but Rueben responded, "How can you say such a thing. Far be it from us, your guests, to do anything like that! We even brought back the money we found in our wallets. So why would we steal from your employer's house?"

"That's right," Simon echoed. "If any of us have this ring, you can imprison him and the rest of us will be the administrator's servants."

"Very well then," the steward said. "Whoever is found to have it will become my administrator's servant. The rest of you will be set free."

The security men removed the luggage from the car and searched each piece, starting with the oldest and ending with the youngest. The ring was found in Benjamin's suitcase.

THE MAKING OF A MAN | 149

"No, how can this be?" Jude shouted. "Benjamin would never take something that wasn't his."

Benjamin denied ever seeing the ring, but the security men ordered them back into the car and returned to Joseph's house.

Joseph was still at the house when Jude and his family arrived. He said to them, "¿Qué clase de gente eres? Es este cualquier forma de tratar un host?" (What kind of people are you? Is this any way to treat a host?)

Jude replied, "What can we say, sir? What can we say? How can we prove our innocence? We cannot! God has uncovered our guilt and is about to punish us for it. We are your servants. Do with us what you want, all of us, including the one who had the ring."

But Joseph said, "Ahora que me castigar a quienes no son culpables! Sólo la que se encuentra que el ladrón se convertirá en mi siervo. El resto de ustedes puede volver a tu padre." (Far be it from me to punish those who are not guilty! Only the one found to be the thief will become my servant. The rest of you may go back to your father.)

*   *   *

Joseph's plan was perfectly orchestrated. While it appeared that he was working a slow revenge on his brothers, his real motivation was not revenge but repentance. Through his schemes, his brothers were coming to an awareness of their guilt and were now close to acknowledging it. Joseph, of course, knew they did not steal his ring, as did his brothers and cousins. When they spoke of God uncovering their guilt, they were coming face-to-face with the cover-up of their sin many years before. It was that terrible sin against their brother that weighed heavily on their father and was a sin against their God. It, like any sin, hung over them and pressed down on them like a heavy weight. Ironically, Joseph's manipulations were steering his family in a way that closely resembled the outcome of their treatment of him. Benjamin was to disappear from Thomas, just as Joseph disappeared, and the rest of the family was to return to their father's home. Joseph's goal was to bring their sins to the surface, acknowledge them, and bring about a healing, a cleansing, and forgiveness in each of their lives.[11]

*   *   *

Jude stepped forward, not defiantly, but humbly, and asked, "Sir, I know that you are as powerful and influential as the president himself. If I may recount what has happened without incurring your anger, I would be grateful."

Joseph nodded affirmatively.

"Sir, you asked us if we had a father or a brother. And we answered, 'We have a father who is growing old.' Actually, he's the father of my cousins who are here. My uncle has a young son born to him in his old age. His mother died giving birth. They had another son before this, but he is dead. This young son, Benjamin, is the only one left of natural birth between them, and he loves Benjamin very much. You, sir, requested that we bring this boy back as a test of our honesty. We told you that our father would die if he lost another son. Nevertheless, you insisted that we do so, or you would not meet with us and Simon would remain in prison.

"We related all this to our father and our uncle, and through prayer, they felt that God wanted us to return, so reluctantly, they allowed Benjamin to return with us, but not without reliving the fact that, as my father put it, 'One of my sons went away from me. He surely must be dead! I have not seen him since. If you take this one from me and harm comes to him, you will drive me to my grave. Do you understand? To my grave in misery!'

"So now if I return without him, I fear for my father's life. I promised my father that I would guarantee the boy's safety. I pledged that if I did not bring him back, I would bear the blame all my life! I want to thank you, sir, for listening and indulging in this long explanation. I beg you then to take me as your servant in place of the boy and let him return with his brothers. Please, do not let me bring that kind of misery upon his father."

---

[11]   Paraphrased from the Expositor's Bible Commentary, Frank E. Gaebelein, vol. 2, p. 254-255.

Joseph could hold himself back no longer. He ordered his staff, "Todo el mundo dejo." (Everyone leave.) Once more, the Zurbriggen/Buchanan family was left in confusion. Joseph fell to his knees and began wailing. His crying was so loud the entire household heard it, and soon, word was delivered to the president of Joseph's emotional outbreak.

Regaining some composure, he looked up at his brothers and cried out, "I am Joseph! I am Joseph! Is my father really alive?"

They all stood paralyzed with shock, unable to answer him as they were terrified with fear.

Joseph got to his feet and waved his arms. "Come! Come close to me."

Slowly and cautiously, they moved toward him. When they approached, he said, "I am your brother Joseph, the one you abandoned in New York. Don't fear and don't be angry with yourselves for what you did. You see, I have learned that God sent me here ahead of you to save lives. Evil men have been willing to kill, maim, and destroy everything good that God has created to satisfy their own lust for power and control over others. God has empowered me to be his instrument against this evil. He sent me here. It was not you. He made me to be second-in-command of all Colombia."

Jude was the first to speak. He said, "Our fathers sent us here to investigate the possibility of sending some of our manufacturing to Colombia. We had no idea you were . . . Is it really you, Joseph?"

"You can see for yourselves, and you have heard what I have said. No one else would know these things. Even my little brother Benjamin knows that I am Joseph." He threw his arms around Benjamin and then hugged each of them.

"You must go and tell my dad what has become of me and tell him that I want him to come here as quickly as he can. We have much lost time to make up."

There was a great celebration among them. Joseph kept hugging his brothers and cousins as if he could not get enough of having his family so close. They carried on into the night laughing and crying with joy over the miracle of God's works.

*   *   *

When news reached President Turlay that Joseph's brothers had come to Colombia primarily to seek a new source of manufacturing but were part of the captives taken during the hostage crisis, he expressed his pleasure over their safe return by inviting Joseph's father and the entire family to Colombia as his guests. He also made his presidential jet available to take the family home and to return for the rest of the family when they were able to accept his invitation. In addition, he contacted leaders in the garment industry and suggested it would be in their best interest to be extremely accommodating to Joseph's family. As a parting gift, Joseph presented each of the young men with the "Best of the Show" garments from the national fashion competition, but to Benjamin, he gave five sets of the winning fashions and cash that amounted to three times what was paid to buy Joseph when he was auctioned off as a slave. The president had made it his business to learn the details of Joseph's abduction and symbolically desired to drive home the point of God's promised blessings. The president sent them off with this admonition: "Don't quarrel on the way!" for he knew they would be debating on the method used to inform their father of Joseph and who should be blamed.

The boys boarded the presidential jet and flew nonstop to Wisconsin. Thomas, Rob, Henrika, and all the grandchildren were there to meet them. The plane had barely stopped when Thomas ran out to meet the boys as they deplaned. Reuben was the first to exit, and he shouted, "Dad, Joseph is alive!" Thomas stopped, thinking he had heard incorrectly, but Reuben shouted again, "Joseph is still alive!" By this time, the other boys were stumbling down the stairs and had gathered around the family.

"I don't believe you. What are you trying to do, give this old man a heart attack?"

"It's true, Dad," Nathan called out. "Joseph is as powerful in Colombia as the president himself. How do you suppose we were able to take the presidential jet home?"

Thomas stood with his jaw hanging open in disbelief. "How did this happen? Oh, for the goodness of the Lord, my son, my son is alive. I must go to see him before I die! Tell me more. Tell me everything," but before they could explain, they were surrounded by a host of reporters, making an explanation impossible. Apparently, news leaked out that the president of Colombia's plane was landing at the Eau Claire Airport. Cameras and microphones were shoved toward the Zurbriggens, followed by a barrage of questions, each begging for answers from a news media that could find no official mention of foreign dignitaries visiting the United States.

Security waded into the frenzy and separated the reporters from the family, and Rob, the ever-ready marketing man, stayed behind. Although he didn't have many details, he was going to make the most of this free exposure. Holding his hand up in front of the reporters, he calmly said, "I'll answer any questions if I have the answer, and if you ask one at a time." He pointed to a reporter from WEAU-TV, giving her an indication to go ahead.

"Sir, what is your name, and what connection do you have to the president of Colombia's plane?"

"I'm Rob Buchanan, vice president of Zurbriggen Classic Wear. Several of those young men that just landed are my sons."

"Mr. Buchanan, could you explain why your sons are being transported by the president's plane?"

"Yes, Mr. Zurbriggen and I sent our sons to Colombia to an International Fashion Show. They were some of the fifty hostages taken captive by the drug lord Pablo Escobar. There are many details that I do not have, but if you would make arrangements with my office, I would be happy to provide more information when it is available."

"Were your sons hurt during the kidnapping, and how did they manage to receive such high-level treatment?"

"This has to do with an abduction of Thomas Zurbriggen's son by Colombian nationals many years ago. Apparently, he has been found alive in Colombia. Further details I do not have at this time. That is all." Rob turned and went into the airport, thinking it wise to leave them with a little teaser.

"Mr. Buchanan, what is the son's name in Colombia. Mr. Buchanan!" the reporters shouted. "Mr. Buchanan . . ."

EPILOGUE

THE STORY YOU have just read is true. The names have been changed to protect you, the reader, from predisposition. The main points within this story originated in the life of a man named Jacob. The original account of his life and that of his family can be seen in Genesis chapter 25 through chapter 47 of the Bible. I changed the names (Jacob becomes Tomas), changed their nationality (from Jewish to Swiss), changed their location (from the Middle East to the Midwest), and changed the time frame (from between 2000 BC and 1800 BC to the 1940s through 1970s).

You may wonder why go to the trouble of contemporizing a historical account. Allow me to explain. When I was a youngster, Biblical stories were just that – stories! I found them very difficult to understand, much less believe. As I approached my thirties, I grew more concerned about the responsibility of leading my children toward what was *truth*. Consequently, I began to examine the Bible with the intent to discover whether it was just fables passed down through generations or if it was factual. My journey earned me the reputation of "The Great Skeptic" because of the barrage of questions I heaped upon those who professed belief in the Holy Scriptures as the inerrant word of God.

I examined the belief tenets of many different religions and found them to be lacking. Even Christianity, in my early opinion, fell into that category. It wasn't until I realized that Christianity had one distinct characteristic that the others did not have – it had a savior who was risen from the dead, whose life was prophesied from the beginning of time, who was referred to thousands of years before appearing on earth, and who promised eternal life in heaven for all who accepted His sentence of death as payment, as a gift in other words, for the wrongs we incurred, that is, our sins.

Even this did not make sense to me at first. Why would anyone want to pay for the gross things that I have done – or for that matter, the lesser things? And further, how would that work? How could one man's death pay for another man's debt? It just did not seem to make sense until I began to measure what my college professors were teaching (evolution) against what the Bible was teaching (creation). Upon close comparison, it became obvious that evolutionary conclusions were provisional upon the amount of data available at the time; and since the data are constantly changing with new discoveries, evolution required its believers to have a great deal of *faith* in a man-made theory.

On the other hand, the Bible is a historical document whose sixty-six books were written by at least forty authors over several thousand years, each independent of one another geographically, economically, and educationally, yet without contradiction. I know for a fact that even within one of the chapters contained in my book, an editor can find errors and contradictions. This uniform connection sets the Bible apart from any other writing. Combine that with the fact that as science "evolved," scientific discoveries have proved occurrences written about in the Bible to be true. These were the same occurrences that were previously scoffed at and labeled by scientists to be fables.

As my studies revealed more evidence of the Bible's authenticity, it became increasingly difficult for me to believe that the world came crashing into existence and out of that slurry mass a single living cell came into being, which evolved into an amphibian creature, which sprouted legs and crawled onto land, eventually grew hair, stood on its hind legs, and, voila, became my relative. Well, if you knew some of my relatives, that last part is almost believable. However, it was still beyond my intellectual ability to understand a supreme being who created not only this world and all its intricacies but also galaxies upon galaxies and was still interested enough in me and you to create a replacement, a substitute who would die for my sins.

I finally concluded that belief required something I did not have – *faith!* The scientists had it, the professors I had in college possessed it, but I didn't have it. It wasn't until I realized *I was not all knowing. I was not omnipotent.* I could not state beyond a shadow of a doubt that my skepticism had merit. It was at that point of honest self-evaluation that I was enlightened. I discovered that God was not going to give me all the answers. He intentionally restricted certain knowledge so that His creation would acknowledge His greatness and accept what was unanswerable by – what was it that I said the professors and scientists possessed? Oh, yes, *faith.* But their faith was in their own intellect. It was a belief in whatever man could devise. It was at this point that I came to the end of myself and accepted what I had learned about God as a tool and accepted what I did not know about God by *faith.*

I realize that many will not go to the Bible and search for answers as I did, but it is my hope that many who read *The Making of a Man* discover the same principles in this contemporary story gleaned from the Bible and apply them as if they had read the Bible. It is also my hope that you, the reader, will come to love and personally know the God who is our creator, the Jesus who is our Savior and who wants us to spend all of eternity with Him in heaven.

I once heard about a queer twist befalling to those professing atheism. It goes something like this:

It is clear that when people declare they are atheists, they are basically stating that they have examined all there is to know in the universe and have concluded **there is no God**.

However, in making such a conclusion, they are stating that they are **all knowing** and by assuming that attribute are declaring **they are God**, which causes the atheist a huge problem because previously they stated **there is no God**; therefore, they, by their own declaration, **do not exist!**

Apply and Multiply – Cliff LeCleir

ABOUT THE AUTHOR

CLIFF LECLEIR'S LIFE began in the simplest of ways, on a Wisconsin farm without electricity, running water, or indoor plumbing. As a youngster, he was constantly involved in creating new ventures in hope of enhancing his savings account. He sold pony rides, raised chickens, using his savings to purchase a cow in order to sell her milk for a steadier income. From the sixth grade, his parents expected him to manage his money in order to provide his own clothes, school supplies, and spending money.

After graduating from high school, he spent three years in the Army, half of which was as a topographer in Ethiopia. Returning to Wisconsin and civilian life, he married, began college, had three children, and began his first business, all in five years.

At the age of 63 he began the 5th business of his career, calling it "*his retirement project.*" Recuperation from hip surgery provided him time to contemplate another venture – *writing!* His writing is plain, down to earth, and from the heart. His first book, *From the Outhouse to the Moon,* has stories surrounding the early days of his life. The second book, *Escape from Tyranny,* is an emotional account of a young couple's escape from Germany in the 1790's. Book three,

The Making of a Man, is a rewrite of a character from ancient Jewish history, but places his character in a contemporary format.

Cliff resides in the rural township of Barre near La Crosse, Wisconsin. His hobbies include using his "toys" (a backhoe, bulldozer and dump truck) to create ponds and waterfalls on his land, cutting wood, teaching adult Bible Classes, and playing racquetball. Now in his 70's he quips, *"I have a plan. When I'm 80, I'm going to slow down – I don't care what anyone says!"*